Sometimes it Happens

W0254613

Sometimes it Happens

KARAN SHARMA

Srishti
PUBLISHERS & DISTRIBUTORS

Srishti Publishers & Distributors
Registered Office: N-16, C.R. Park
New Delhi – 110 019
Corporate Office: 212A, Peacock Lane
Shahpur Jat, New Delhi – 110 049
editorial@srishtipublishers.com

First published by Notion Press in 2017

Revised version, 2019
First published by
Srishti Publishers & Distributors in 2019

Copyright © Karan Sharma, 2019

10 9 8 7 6 5 4 3 2 1

This is a work of fiction. The characters, places, organisations and events described in this book are either a work of the author's imagination or have been used fictitiously. Any resemblance to people, living or dead, places, events or organisations is purely coincidental.

The author asserts the moral right to be identified as the author of this work.

All rights reserved. No part of this publication may be reproduced, stored in a retrieval system, or transmitted, in any form or by any means, electronic, mechanical, photocopying, recording or otherwise, without the prior written permission of the Publishers.

Printed and bound in India

Acknowledgments

THE CREATIVE *KEEDA* IN ME HAS BEEN THERE SINCE birth. I always wanted to do something different and not follow the trodden path, and I have to thank my parents, Baldevkrishan Sharma and Promila Sharma, for letting me be myself always and giving me a great platform to work on. My grandparents, Sushiladevi Sharma and Ram Ratan Sharma, have had a great influence on my life, and to whom I will remain eternally thankful.

My story writing will always be dedicated to my mother, who is an avid movie fan and never misses catching every new Hindi movie. Though I am not handsome enough to be a Bollywood star, I do hope to recreate the magic of movies for her through the stories I write. This gift of writing is a result of her blessings, but the creativity in my work is a gift I have inherited from my father, who is an avid poet himself.

This book would have never seen the light of day, had it not been for my beautiful wife, Aarti, and her dedication to making my two sons, Aakash and Aayansh, read the hundreds of books she collects for them. She has been the greatest supporter of my creativity and whatever success I achieve, I owe to her.

My sister, Mona Menon, has been a pillar of strength and a great partner in business; my brother-in-law, Pratap Menon; elder brother, Rajesh Tara, and bua, Tripta Sharma, have been my support system throughout my life. I thank all my in-law families – the super cool Gulatis, Chandhokes, Alimchandanis, and Vithalanis – whose encouragement and love I cherish the most. Among them, special thanks to Shreya Gulati for being the first person to read my story and give her frank feedback, which helped to make this book even better. I also thank Kunal Gulati for his inputs while editing the book.

I acknowledge Vandana Sethhi for her promotion inputs for the book.

This chapter in my life as an author is with Srishti Publishers whom I thank for giving me a break and bringing me into the folds of traditional publishing. To get such backing from a publishing powerhouse is truly appreciated.

Finally, I thank god for blessing and guiding me and for making this book really happen.

IT WAS A PERFECT WINTER'S DAY IN MUMBAI, THE financial capital of India and the hub of the banking industry, stock exchanges and of course, Bollywood. Being an island city, Mumbai did not get very cold and the temperature that day hovered just below thirty degrees Celsius. Mumbai, truth be told, has only three types of climate – peak summer, moderate summer with rains and mild summer. The city that day was glistening with bright sunshine, with birds chirping and a slight south westerly breeze blowing.

The energy of the city is something to behold, with more than twenty million people crammed into it. It is the city of dreams with many stories of rags to riches – people turning into millionaires and billionaires in a matter of few years with extreme hard work and a little luck, of course.

Out of the window on the tenth floor of a modern light blue residential building, one could see, on one side the beautiful Shivaji Park, one of the few remaining open grounds in the city where the greatest batsman of all times, Sachin Tendulkar learnt his trade, under his coach, Padma Shri Dronacharya award recipient Ramakant Achrekar Sir. And on the other side, the calm Arabian Sea, with the new icon of Mumbai, the stringed Bandra-Worli Sea Link bridge, standing proudly over it.

Two crows, an avian species commonly found all over Mumbai, had become special friends of Rohit over the years as they often acted as his wake up alarm. Their constant cawing finally woke him from the deep slumber he was in. It had been another night out for Rohit, a twenty-five-year-old MBA graduate and a banker in a multinational bank called Global Bank. For Rohit, nights-out were an important part of the routine to keep his youthful adrenaline flowing. It did not matter whether it was a weekday or a weekend; he just could not say no to a party. This particular night had gone on for a longer time than expected, and by the time he hit the bed, he was too sleepy to set the alarm.

Rohit, originally from Delhi, had shifted to Mumbai at the beginning of his college days. His father had been transferred there after becoming the managing director of India's biggest national bank. So smitten was Rohit with Mumbai, the city that never sleeps, that he decided to stay back when his entire family shifted back to Delhi. Given his smooth-talking ways, he had been able to get an amazing two-bedroom apartment from his father in central Mumbai, close to his swanky office building located in Bandra Kurla Complex, more popularly known as BKC. It had become the nerve centre of the banking industry, with majority of the banks having their head offices there.

Rohit, with eyes still red, placed his iPhone in its docking station to belt out the latest Bollywood songs and hurriedly got into the cold shower. The room was a mess like any bachelor pad, with clothes strewn all over, dust in every nook and corner and every piece of furniture having a pair of shoes lying beside it.

His house was cleaned and tidied only on Sundays every week after the Saturday night parties at his place. The only silver lining about the mess was how quickly Rohit could dress up and find his shoes as if he telepathically knew where all his stuff lay. He quickly gulped down the milk from his fridge without even checking its expiry date. He did, however, notice the sour aftertaste. With breakfast done, it was time to leave.

Out hurried Rohit from his building, smartly dressed in a blue shirt with a bright red tie, which reflected his vibrant, youthful personality and beige trousers, all set to begin a new day in office. Already late for work and the peak office hours coinciding with his own, he could not find any app-based cabs around. Luckily, he found a traditional black and yellow taxi of the famed Italian brand, Fiat.

One has to be especially careful when getting into these cabs, to avoid touching any side of the doors, so as to save oneself from greasing and dirtying one's clothes. Rohit got in with utmost care. Once seated, he called his best friend and colleague, Gautam, to check his whereabouts.

"I already reached the office an hour ago," replied Gautam.

"What the hell are you doing there so early?" asked a surprised Rohit.

"I had some practice to do, but don't ask me what it is. You come here and I'll tell you," replied Gautam in a nervous tone and hurriedly hung up.

Rohit was left exasperated and confused while starting to wonder what his best friend was hiding from him. Was it an important conference call that Rohit had missed? Was it their annual assessment or evaluation or appraisal? Was a downsizing of the team happening? Was he about to be culled? Rohit's imagination was going haywire.

The taxi slowly made its way through the heavy morning traffic, honking merrily. Rohit was so lost in his own thoughts wondering about Gautam that he failed to notice his beautiful colleague Payal, dressed in a frilled pink shirt with deep blue trousers and a matching smart, deep blue jacket waving to him from across the road. Payal, who was the same age as him, had been Rohit's colleague for the last couple of years but they weren't too friendly with each other. Payal believed Rohit was an over-the-top guy who would do anything to get his work done and his suaveness irritated her no end. On the other hand, Rohit found Payal too reserved and career-driven. Her aloofness and serious outlook irked him.

Payal had been desperately trying to get Rohit's attention but to no avail. She came from an upper middle-class background and would usually take an autorickshaw to work as her place was a short distance away. Unfortunately, she could not get hold of a single one that day. She was happy to spot Rohit in the taxi, certain she could share the ride. Finally she gave up waiting to get Rohit's reaction and, after a short sprint from the bus stop where she was standing, she hopped into the back seat of the taxi.

"What is wrong with you, Rohit? I was waving at you madly, and you did not even notice. Were you ignoring me deliberately?" asked an angry Payal trying to maintain her calm.

Noticing Rohit's clueless and dazed expression, she sensed something was amiss.

"What happened? Did another girl reject you?" asked Payal with a mischievous smile, trying to irritate Rohit – and succeeding.

"That, Payal, will sadly never happen." Rohit frowned, not wanting to discuss his personal relationships with her, and continued, "It's something about Gautam. He is in the office so early and will not even tell me why."

"Aren't you and Gautam very close friends?" asked Payal probingly.

"Yes, we go a long way back. We studied in the same college, did our MBA together and now even work side by side. We have been through thick and thin. Since the time I shifted to Mumbai ten years ago, we have always been there for each other," Rohit replied.

"Wow, that is some friendship," replied an impressed Payal. "But how different are the two of you!" Payal did not want to lose the opportunity to rub Rohit the wrong way.

She continued, "Gautam is a reserved person, while you never know when to keep quiet. You flirt with every girl who comes into your sight while he speaks with so much respect to everyone."

Rohit however was not the kind of a person who could be flustered by criticism. He had become used to it.

With a smirk on his face, Rohit replied, "You see, Gautam is not what he seems. He will be polite to your face, but that is not necessarily what he is really like. You know, the nerdy silent type. With me, on the other hand, you get what you see."

"Then what I see is surely not appreciable," teased Payal and burst out laughing, as a red-faced Rohit shook his head in disgust.

The taxi came to a stop outside their plush corporate building, which was reflecting the bright sunlight.

Rohit rushed out of the taxi, casually strolled next to the driver and remarked while pointing at Payal, "Bro, the kind-hearted madam will pay the fare." Then, he started walking away, to Payal's utmost shock as she gathered her things in the taxi.

"Where the hell is your chivalry, Mr Rohit?" asked an infuriated Payal in a stern voice as she stuck her face out of the window.

"Gave it to Gautam for rent. Collect the taxi fare from him, then maybe, you will be able to see his generosity as well," Rohit said sarcastically in a calm voice and coolly walked away.

Rohit entered the office building, and after swiping his identity card at the security check, he took the lift to the second floor. The designated floor was designed keeping in mind the latest trends in interiors, with stress put on open spaces and bright colours. The entire floor of around ten thousand square feet was filled with individual cubicles clustered together and a couple of private glass conference rooms at the end of the floor. This is where Rohit, Payal, and Gautam had their cubicles overlooking the busy main road.

Stepping out of the lift, Rohit, to his surprise, found a small crowd gathered at the back of the office floor near one of the conference rooms.

He was now even more baffled and inquired about the reason for the commotion, as he continued to make his way to the back. But no one was ready to respond to him, as they were glued to the centre of the action.

The public address system of the conference room was on, and Rohit recognised a familiar voice.

He immediately climbed onto a desk to get a clearer view.

His eyes widened and jaw suddenly dropped. He could not believe what he was seeing –

Gautam, fair-skinned, with a six-foot, three-inch frame and lean body, was on his knees with a rose in hand, seemingly proposing to Ms Breganza, a healthy sixty-year-old lady assistant to their director.

"I LOVE YOU FROM THE BOTTOM OF MY HEART AND WILL not take no for an answer," Gautam said with utmost sincerity to a shocked Ms Breganza, who had turned white in fear, wondering what was coming up next.

Gautam continued his love professing, "Yes, I have loved you since the first day my eyes fell on you and want to spend the rest of my life with you. I will love you as long as…" Gautam cleared his throat, "you live," he said at his romantic best, with a charming face and in a confident voice that tapered off at the end.

He had no clue that the speaker in the conference room had been accidentally switched on and that the entire office was watching and hearing his proposal in shock. There was pin-drop silence outside as everyone wanted to catch every word Gautam spoke. Rohit was still standing on the desk, rubbing his eyes in disbelief.

"As long as I live, my foot," thundered Ms Breganza. "I don't want to see you henceforth!" she shouted, her face boiling with anger, as she began to leave.

Gautam, now desperate and oblivious to the growing crowd outside, caught her feet and begged her, "What is wrong with me? I will be an ideal–"

Before he could finish his sentence, she kicked him hard and left the room hurriedly without looking back at Gautam, who was seething in pain – physical, not emotional, .

As Gautam came out of the conference room, everyone on the floor burst out in laughter, with whistles and cheers going around. Realising that so many people had been watching him, Gautam turned red with embarrassment. He could see women shaking their heads in disgust, while the men, laughing uncontrollably, came forward to pat his back. Gautam had come across to his colleagues as a thoroughly serious person, only interested in working and climbing up the corporate ladder. But this incident, he knew, would have dented their outlook towards him forever.

Gautam saw Rohit climbing down from the table and coming towards him with a 'what were you thinking' look. He thought of a quick idea about how to save himself from the humiliating situation he had found himself in. He was even prepared to sacrifice his best friend, Rohit, for that.

Gautam shouted loudly so that he could be heard by all, "There, Rohit! Take the five hundred bucks. I've lost this bet with you." Gautam shrugged innocently and continued, "Ms Breganza turned down my proposal. She did not even take me seriously."

Gautam knew that, with the kind of reputation Rohit had, no one would have been surprised by such a wager, and that was the only way he could save face.

Rohit readily grabbed the money to Gautam's dismay, knowing very well that given his situation Gautam had no other option but to let it go. However, he still could not control his laughter.

He shook his head and put a hand around his longtime buddy. "I know, you used to fantasize about beautiful older women, but this is too much. With this act of yours, you have put me under a lot of stress. Now, I will have to even tell my mom to stay away from you. You disgusting man," Rohit continued his uncontrollable laughter. "Gautam, what desperation made you do this? It isn't even the first of April today," he remarked with a shake of his head.

Before Gautam could reply, he heard a voice of support.

"Leave him alone, Rohit," quipped Payal. "You have already spoiled my day with your smart ass behaviour. At least spare your best friend the cheap humour."

Payal had a soft spot for Gautam and was quick to defend him. Even though she had not witnessed the proposal, she vouched for Gautam's innocence.

Rohit had tried hitting on Payal a couple years ago when she had joined the bank. She had made it amply clear to him that her employment was to further her career and not create love stories or flirt with men. This episode was the cornerstone of their cold relationship, and ever since, neither ever let go of an opportunity to embarrass the other.

Before Rohit could use his big quota of snide remarks to retort to Payal, who had already started walking away, Gautam put his hand on Rohit's mouth and pulled him away.

"I will tell you the truth, Rohit," said Gautam in a dejected voice while nodding his head. He took Rohit to one corner of the office and confessed in a low voice, "Listen, I was practicing my proposal technique and believed it would be better to try it on an old aunty who at least would not reject me. It would give me immense confidence and self-belief to make the final proposal without fear, I thought. I even literally begged her, and you saw that, Rohit." Gautam threw up his arms in dismay. "She still refused. Damn it. I don't know what else I was supposed to do."

They started walking together towards their desks. Rohit, though, was not done questioning him and was still confused about the whole event.

"So whom are you going to propose next, to further boost your confidence?" queried Rohit in a light-hearted and sarcastic way.

"I guess it will be Roshni now," replied Gautam calmly.

"You mean *the* Ms Roshni? Wow, dude, you are descending the age ladder fast! First a sixty-year-old woman and now a forty-year-old. You are a strange man, Gautam. Before this proposal fiasco, I thought I knew you well. I don't know what has gone in to you today."

"She is not forty," retorted Gautam defensively. "She is thirty-seven."

"Thirty-seven. Is that your defence, Gautam? So what? You still surprise me." Rohit could not believe what he had heard from his best friend. He continued, "You may be a good colleague to her, but that's about it. After this proposal, she will not only break your work relationship but will also ensure that you are thrown out of the company. You do realise, she is our Senior Vice President."

With this, Rohit, who was now seated on the chair in his cubicle next to Gautam's, pulled himself to the desk and away from Gautam's view. Only a small partition divided the good friends.

Rohit's eyes suddenly lit up, which was never a good sign, and he pulled his chair back to face Gautam.

Gautam, on the other hand, was sitting silently, lost in his thoughts. The incident in the morning had embarrassed him no end. He had to meet and apologise to Ms Breganza for the entire episode. Sweating furiously, his white shirt had begun showing patches. He looked back at Rohit, rolled his eyes and threw his head back.

"No, Rohit, I know that look of yours. Please, I beg of you, don't say anything," pleaded Gautam, with his hands folded.

Rohit, oblivious to Gautam's pleas, burst out laughing. "Wait, hear me out. With Ms Roshni, there may be another scenario. She is single, if my information is not wrong, and if she thinks you are serious and says yes, you are doomed man, absolutely doomed. I know she is beautiful and kind of hot, which leaves me baffled to why she is still unmarried. But what if she says yes..." Rohit again exploded with his bout of evil laughter.

"It will be so much fun. Just let me know when you are doing it, I will be there. Will not miss it for sure. It will be like those India v/s Pakistan matches, where there is so much suspense, nervous energy and we don't know which way the result is going to go. I want a front row seat to that action."

"Will you just shut up for a minute and be serious?" pleaded Gautam. "With Roshni, it is not going to be practice. It's the real thing."

He pulled out a small box from his shirt pocket and opened it for Rohit to see a glittering, diamond-studded ring. Rohit was stunned as his eyes opened wide in shock.

"I am going to ask her to marry me and will gift her this diamond ring," Gautam remarked in a serious and sincere tone.

ROHIT WAS COMPLETELY TAKEN ABACK. HE WAS IN shock, looking at the glittering diamond ring that Gautam was holding out. In disbelief, he could not even utter a word for a minute.

After a moment of silence which seemed like an eternity, he finally spoke up.

"Bro, are you serious? You have to be kidding me. Tell me this is a joke!" Rohit's voice went from calm to shrill. "Do you realise what you are about to do? This is like an earthquake of massive proportions."

Gautam realised that Rohit's reaction was getting unnecessary attention from the rest of their colleagues around them, so he gestured to Rohit to accompany him to the cafeteria.

They entered the cafeteria, which was relatively empty, considering it was early in the morning – perfect for the friends to discuss their personal issues privately without drawing much attention. Rohit was still in a state of shock and shaking his head in bewilderment. Gautam ordered some tea for both of them. They sat at the end of the cafeteria, which was their favourite hangout place to get away from the pressures of work.

Rohit had two issues flaring up in his mind: first, he could not believe that Gautam was thinking of marriage at the age of twenty-five and second and more importantly, the big age difference between the Gautam and Roshni. It was not normal. One sometimes sees older men married to younger women, but not the other way around. Just thinking about it was so weird and repulsive. Rohit wanted to get to the bottom of this.

Rohit opened up and fired his first salvo.

"Dude, is she pregnant with your child?"

Now it was Gautam's turn to be shocked. "What the hell?" he shouted back, a bit annoyed.

Rohit continued his bizarre theory to make sense of the whole thing.

"Or you just had sex with her, and you are feeling guilty about it? I know you really well, Gautam. You just get sentimental too fast. This time, you have gone mental, as well."

Gautam quickly rebutted his best friend's claim. "What rubbish are you speaking? I just love her, and that is why I want to marry her. Not because of any of your stupid reasons."

Gautam took a deep breath and sipped his tea, taking a moment to think about what he was about to disclose. He had been keeping some things from his close friend, and it was time he came clean.

He started his explanation. "To tell you the truth, Rohit, I have not been totally honest with you about my relationship with Roshni. We have been seeing each other and dating for the past three months now."

Gautam was already preparing himself for the backlash from Rohit.

"What? I am your best friend, and you only tell me this now? What kind of a friend are you?" asked a baffled and angry Rohit, completely startled at this revelation.

Gautam defended himself to make Rohit see sense in the decision of not letting him in on his love secret earlier. "I was expecting this kind of reaction from you and hence I had decided to tell you later. Even I did not know where our relationship was headed and whether we were serious. Was it just a crush I had, or just a fling for both of us? But now, I know that it is love for sure, and I want to marry her and be with her for the rest of my life. I want to spend every day of my life with her and share everything. I want to have children with her. I can't think of not having her as a big part of my life anymore."

Gautam had expressed his feelings in a truly honest and sincere way, hoping to get Rohit to understand him. However, his friend was not yet ready to give in to Gautam's emotional appeal. He continued his tirade against his dear friend.

"All this time when you made excuses like you were doing some work-related research, bonding with your parents whom you were supposedly meeting less frequently due to long working hours, not feeling well, having frequent stomach upsets and meeting your long lost school friends... whenever I called you to hang out, you were blatantly lying to my face? Damn. Only a girl – and in your case a woman – could have come between our friendship. I hate it when men like you try to manipulate things because of a certain woman," said Rohit in a clearly cynical and disgruntled voice. With seething anger written all over his face, he continued, "So anyway, why are you informing me about this now? Why did you not directly invite me to your wedding? I am assuming you are telling me now because you need something from me."

"My dearest Rohit," Gautam replied sympathetically, understanding the justified anger of his friend. "Will you cool it now? Dude, I am really sorry, but at this moment I need your support, not backlash."

"Okay, okay. Now comes the senti friendship crap. So like I predicted, you indeed need something from me. What is that you want?" asked an angry Rohit.

Gautam felt a bit guilty, but he needed his friend's support. "I have not told my parents yet, and I am expecting they will freak out when I finally do, as any Indian parent would."

"What about your sister, does she know?" asked Rohit, who was slowly giving into Gautam's persistence and warming up to helping his best friend in his hour of need. "She will be able to convince your parents far better than me. She convinced them about her love marriage; I am sure she can do it for you too. Besides, I don't think your parents value my judgment too well, especially when it comes to women."

"Am I missing something here?" asked a puzzled Gautam. "Did something happen between you and my parents I am not aware of?"

"I did not tell you this as it was particularly embarrassing," replied Rohit sheepishly, "but I guess you need to know now."

"This happened around a year back. I was standing at the counter of a pharmacy in Bandra, wondering loudly which condom brand to buy. 'Which one should I take? Kamasutra or Moods? Kamasutra or Moods…'

Without looking at the face of the elderly man standing right next to me, I nudged him and asked coolly, 'Uncle, you seem to be highly experienced. Which should I choose Moods or Kamasutra?'

It was then that my eyes fell upon the man whom I had just asked for advice and to my utmost shock, it turned out to be your father and standing right next to him was your mother.

'Two strips of Saridon, please,' I improvised to save face, asking the shopkeeper sheepishly.

Then I again turned towards your parents, my face red, flushed with embarrassment. 'I was just getting some medicine, Uncle.'

I thought that it would be the end of the conversation, but no, your father had other thoughts. "What kind of thing does Moods cure, son?" he asked with a straight face.

'Moods is for…' I obviously stumbled, searching for the right words. I could not think of something, so I asked the chemist, 'Sir, what is Moods used for?' in the most innocent tone I could.

The chemist nonchalantly replied, without giving a damn about my predicament, 'They're condoms.'

'Condom…' a nervous laugh came out of me, and so did the next line. 'And now you will tell me that Kamasutra are also condoms.'

'Yes,' was the instant reply from the chemist.

I had to save the situation for myself, as it was just going from bad to worse.

'Uncle, your son is so mischievous. I asked him to suggest a medicine for the pain in my leg and look what he did. He is a very funny person, indeed. Anyway, I will take your leave now. Gautam is waiting in the car.' I ran away from the scene as fast as I could."

Now it was Gautam's turn to get annoyed with his best friend Rohit.

"You screwed me so badly, dude. Because of you, my nightlife was destroyed for a month. I had no clue why my parents were so intense with me. They even started plotting my marriage. They thought I was sleeping with every woman I knew," laughed Gautam, as he got up from his chair.

It was a bittersweet moment for Gautam. He had finally become aware of the reason behind his parents' strange behaviour and could not believe that his best friend was the one responsible for it. On the other hand the incident itself was so hilarious that he couldn't help but laugh it off.

Gautam put his hand out to Rohit. "Let's call it even and move forward."

Rohit reluctantly accepted the handshake as he knew he had no other option. What was done was done. "No secrets from here on," Rohit proposed, and Gautam accepted it with a smile.

They started to walk back to their workstations.

"On a serious note," Gautam continued, "you are the only one who knows Roshni well. So you will have to plead along with me for her, to my parents. I will be indebted to you for the rest of my life, if you are able to convince them. I love them a lot, and don't want to marry anyone without their consent for sure."

"Yes, I know," Rohit agreed. "However, for me to convince your parents, one thing is necessary. I have to be first convinced myself that what you are doing is right." Rohit turned around and looked Gautam straight in the eye. "And by the way, given the big age difference of twelve years between you both, have you really really thought this through with a straight, logical mind?"

"SO, HOW DO YOU WANT TO BE CONVINCED?" ASKED Gautam, brimming with confidence. "Would three or four punches do the trick or do I have to pin you to the ground?" Gautam, with his tall and decently built body, obviously had an advantage over the leaner and slightly shorter Rohit.

"Save the trash talk for some other day, Gautam, not on a day when you want me to help you," replied Rohit with his snobbish smile. "Let's go out for lunch to the new Chinese restaurant, 'China Valley,' around the corner. Of course, your treat."

They both agreed to meet at 2:00 p.m. for lunch to take this conversation forward. Gautam wanted to prove his love to Rohit, who on the other hand, wanted to make sure that his best friend had thought his decision through.

At two they made the short walk from their office to the plush new Chinese restaurant. Once seated, Rohit, in his extravagant style, ordered the restaurant's specialties without even looking at the menu. He was not going to let Gautam go lightly, especially when he had the upper hand.

With Chinese tea in one hand and a dim sum in the other, Rohit started off. "You only have to convince me that your decision is rational and my support will be unconditional thereafter."

"Okay. So shoot whatever you want to ask me, and I will answer everything honestly to prove my love," replied Gautam confidently.

Gautam was looking forward to this question-format conversation with Rohit as he thought this would prepare him well for the discussion he would eventually have with his parents. If he could clear Rohit's line of questioning with flying colours, he could clear anything after that, he thought to himself.

"What makes you feel your initial fling has converted into a serious relationship? Has she given you any hints?" Rohit fired his first friendly question.

"Well, it's the way we speak to each other and how open and frank we both are. She wants to know about my childhood and college days. She has seen the photos as well. Any woman interested in a long-term relationship always does this. We discuss the future in terms of our respective careers, discuss our personal matters – all things that a normal couple in love will talk about. We have spent hours together speaking on the phone and have probably shared everything about our lives with each other. We have also been on long drives, day picnics and generally spent some amazing quality time together," replied Gautam, his eyes lost in thinking about Roshni and the good times they had shared. A smile appeared on his face while relating the experience – a sign of true love.

But Rohit was not one whose heart would melt so easily. He had faced a lot of breakups in his life, giving him a neutral view of Gautam's feelings. His flurry of questions continued nonchalantly, while eating the delicious dim sums. "Are you physically attracted to her as you would be to, let's say, a twenty-four-year-old girl?"

"You bet I am, without a shadow of a doubt. She does not even look her age. If I had not known it, I would have passed her off as someone in her late twenties or early thirties," replied Gautam promptly with a sense of pride in his voice.

Rohit looked at Gautam with a shocked face before breaking into a mischievous smile. "I totally agree, man. She is extremely hot."

That reply had Gautam throwing his napkin at Rohit's face in disgust. "You idiot, you are talking about my to-be wife here."

"I was just appreciating her, dude, take it easy," Rohit shot back in his calm and collected way with a grin on his face.

"Tell me, Gautam, what is the hurry to get married so early, when you are only twenty-five years old? You are just three months into this relationship, so why the eagerness in getting married so quickly?" asked Rohit.

"Rohit, this relationship is unlike any other. I am so sure you have never experienced something like it. I am not saying that I will get married to her immediately – maybe a year down the line – but this proposal will be proof of my commitment to her. I have never felt like this for any woman, and I simply don't want to lose her. I have found the right woman and I am madly in love with her. Does it matter whether I marry her now or three years later?" replied Gautam with love and sincerity reflecting through his words.

The discussion was flowing in the manner of two boxers feeling themselves slowly into a match before the big punches start to fly.

The main course came upon them – a big portion of the delicious burnt garlic fried rice with mapo tofu, a spicy delicacy of the Sichuan preparation.

Rohit's questioning continued. "Do you see yourself, five years down the line, having a family with her?"

"Yes, I do," replied a confident Gautam, happily nibbling on his portion of rice and tofu. "She has so much maturity in handling every situation. When I am around her, I feel so secure and comfortable. I don't know about how good I am going to be as a father but I can assure you that she is going to be an amazing mother."

"So basically you get a motherly treatment from her. My Gautam baby is never going to miss his mom," remarked Rohit with a sympathetic and sarcastic tone both rolled into one. Gautam threw a blank expression at Rohit acknowledging that this was a remark he was very well expecting from him given the age difference.

"Okay, those were the simple questions. Now to start the more uncomfortable ones. Really think hard before you answer these. No rushed answers required," warned Rohit, with a touch of seriousness in his tone.

"You said you wanted her to be the mother of your children, right?" asked Rohit.

"Two, to be precise," added Gautam. "A daughter as beautiful as Roshni, and a son as smart and handsome as me."

Rohit nodded in appreciation. "Excellent, Gautam. Ideal

family, that. Now tell me, when do you think you will want to become a father? I mean age-wise."

Gautam thought long and hard before answering his friend's question. "My career is still taking off, so I will marry her after a year. Then, you know, is the settling, discovering and a romantic phase, which lasts around two to three years. So maybe the first child will be in five years and the second with a minimum gap of three years." Gautam happily answered this query, as he could imagine his future married life before him.

Rohit put his fork down on hearing this and clapped for his friend. "Great planning, Gautam," applauded Rohit with a hint of sarcasm in his voice. "You know as per your plan she will be forty-two years old by the time you have the first child and forty-five by the time the second one comes around. For your information, women generally have problems conceiving children after the age of forty, I hear even after thirty-five. So that gives you three years from now, tops. Which means that, immediately after marriage, you need to have children and hope they are twins. So not much of a romantic phase and there also goes your dream of having two children." A hissing Rohit continued, "This is only your first perfect dream gone bust, man, and I already see you sweating."

"I am not at all having second thoughts. You go on, Rohit," requested a calm looking Gautam.

And so, Rohit's barrage continued. "So let us assume you have one child. You are twenty-eight, and Roshni is forty when he or she is born. Let's assume for the sake of this question that a beautiful daughter is born. She is great at her studies, a brilliant student–"

"Just like me," butted in Gautam, full of pride.

"And believe it or not, she tops the tenth standard in her school," continued Rohit.

"What? School? No way! Look, she will top Mumbai University," interrupted a pumped up Gautam.

"Okay, she does," agreed Rohit with a roll of his eyes. "Then, there is a ceremony to honour her achievement, organised at the school, where the media also wants to interview her. The parents are full of pride. But the daughter, on the other hand, is embarrassed."

There was silence, with Gautam sporting a confused look, wondering the reason for such a prophecy.

"At this point in time, you are supposed to ask me why," bellowed Rohit, pointing a finger at Gautam.

"Okay. Please tell me, Your Highness. Why?" It was Gautam's turn to taunt now.

"Embarrassed because she has to take the stage with her parents. The father being forty-two years and still handsome and her mother, who now looks more like her grandmother, aged fifty-four with white hair. She suffers this awkwardness throughout her school and college days, and this topic is also the butt of many jokes directed towards her. She cannot forgive her parents ever for this." Rohit ended his prediction on a sad note.

After a moment of silence, Gautam retorted, "Rohit, you are just the king of exaggeration. There is something called emotional bonding and love between parents and their child. I think that will surpass any kind of uneasy situation, assuming there even is one."

"I am just putting forth various scenarios and opening your eyes to all kinds of possibilities that you and your family may face in the future. Before you take the crucial step of proposing to her, just think about it with a calm mind. What's the hurry? I am just trying to be a good friend and help you make the right decision. Can I continue with my questions or are you already uncomfortable?" Rohit enquired before proceeding further. On getting a pensive nod from Gautam, he continued.

"You said, and I totally agree, that she is an exceptionally attractive lady. You also agree with me, then, that sex is an important bond in marriage. It brings you both close together and lets your passion do the talking," Rohit took the discussion further.

"For once, I completely agree with you on this," confessed Gautam with a smile, not knowing what Rohit was going to hit him with next.

"Well, then, let's imagine this scenario. You are forty-eight years old, still full of passion and vigour, while she is sixty and, sorry to say—with half a foot in the grave. You think she will have any sex drive left by then? Forget sixty, even when she is fifty-five years old, she will not be able to match your drive, which will only leave you frustrated and tempt you to cheat on her." Rohit had a slight smirk on his face as if he knew he had managed to get into Gautam's mind to make him rethink the relationship. He only had good intentions for his friend and wanted him to think his decision through.

"Anyway, just for your information, Gautam, men around the age of forty-five are most likely to cheat on their wives of the similar age because they feel their sex drive is not good enough for them. And you want to marry a woman who, within five years of marriage, will reach that stage?"

GAUTAM WAS GROWING MORE AND MORE PENSIVE WITH every word Rohit was uttering. He just wanted to shut him up, but he knew deep inside his heart that they were all valid points to think about.

Rohit could, on the other hand, see that the conversation was making Gautam nervous and uncomfortable. But he was in no mood to back down and decided to further push the boundary.

He continued in his exuberant style. "And this is not all. There are even deeper issues. You are a young guy. You like to go clubbing, go to parties, lounges, frequent late nights, dinners with friends – just all the things that a normal twenty-five-year-old man is interested in doing. But the big question is whether she is going to be comfortable with it. Will she be able to match your energy levels for life? Will any of her friends be comfortable around us? Or rather, will she be comfortable being around us young guns? Will our thought processes match? I don't think we will have too many common subjects to discuss."

Gautam looked ready to answer, but Rohit's volley of questions continued unabated. "What if she says you can party only on alternate weekends? And that too, with the condition that you have to be back home before midnight. I hope you know where I am going with all of this."

While spraying his questions, Rohit had wiped his plate clean of the delicious food.

Rohit asked Gautam to think long and hard about all the questions he had put forward and excused himself from the table to freshen up. When he was out of Gautam's sight, he took out a piece of paper from his pocket and looked through the notes he had made of all the points, he needed to discuss. Rohit might have seemed casual, but he was thorough when it came to work. He patted himself on the back for getting through most of the queries, with just a couple remaining to be ticked off.

Gautam, on the other hand, had lost a bit of his appetite. Before Rohit could come back, he got his half-eaten plate picked up by the waiter in a hurry. He did not want to give Rohit any brownie points for all the mayhem he had created.

Their appetites were going in opposite directions. It seemed that with every question, Rohit's hunger was increasing and Gautam's was proportionally decreasing. Rohit was not done yet though, and he went on to order his favourite dessert – caramel custard. Gautam, on the other hand, excused himself from eating anything sweet citing diet control.

Rohit took Gautam's permission and restarted his scenario-creation. "Just imagine yourself sitting at home with her all the time, watching TV or reading books while we party the night out. Can you live with that? In the first three months of dating, you have only been chatting with her on the phone, going for dinners, drives, and on picnics. These are not the things that we young people do. Can you continue to do all these things that people above thirty-five years do?"

This question had made Gautam ponder over the last three months with Roshni. They indeed had spent a lot of time talking and dining and had avoided clubbing and partying. Roshni had preferred not to go to any loud places and Gautam had been all right with this decision. He was completely smitten by her and being a gentleman to the core, adhered to all her requests. Rohit's question though opened a Pandora's box for Gautam. Was he overly changing himself for her? Would he be able to sustain such a lifestyle on long term basis?

Rohit continued his barrage of probing thoughts. "Being elder, she will also dominate you in every decision-making process, be it going out on a vacation, where to dine, which movie to see, what career decisions to make, and so on. It will be no different a situation than it is now while staying with your parents. Roshni will just be a replacement for your mom, in fact worse."

Rohit's caramel custard made its appearance and was gone in no time. While Rohit was relishing the dessert, Gautam, on the other hand, was relishing the silence and a peaceful moment to himself.

But not for too long. Rohit resumed the conversation. "You know, Gautam, marriage is all about companionship, especially when you become old. Since you both belong to two separate generations, over the years, you will start having differences of opinion on every issue. It is obvious, whether you like it or not."

The lecture continued to flow from Rohit. "A husband and wife are supposed to be the best of companions for each other, especially during old age when your children are away for higher studies or work, and your friends have either moved away or have their own health problems to deal with. I should not be saying this, but do you think she will be with you in your old age? At that point in time, to whom would you look for companionship? A younger female? Now that will be the real irony of your life." Rohit's sarcasm was getting on Gautam's nerves, but he maintained his composure.

Rohit finally had a tone of sobriety, as if he was about to throw a knockout punch at his friend. "Listen, Gautam, I am your best friend, and I have only your best interests in mind. I am just not convinced that you have completely thought this through. I do not blame you because you are currently blind in love and that is clouding your judgment. So someone needs to think straight for you, and I have done that. Reflect on all these scenarios and debate them within yourself before you finally decide on the next step. In the end, it is your life."

Gautam, all this while, was getting more and more depressed, imagining the various situations Rohit had narrated. One could see it on his face. All the while, listening to Rohit, he had started developing doubts about his rationale for proposing to Roshni.

"You know, you should meet your sister, Richa, and also discuss this topic with her. Maybe she can be of better help than me," advised Rohit. "She can probably bring an altogether different perspective to you which even I did not think of. This should help you make a better and more informed decision."

"Oh yes, thanks for reminding me. I am, in fact, meeting her in fifteen minutes," replied Gautam in a low voice, after a quick look at his watch. "I don't want to be late. You know how angry she gets. Please do me a favour, buddy and cover for me in the office. I will be back within an hour."

Gautam, as promised, swiped his credit card to pay the bill. On the way out, Rohit could not resist picking up a fortune cookie, as was the tradition in many Chinese restaurants. He quickly opened it up to see what lay ahead of him. 'A friend asks only for your time, not your money.'

"Wow, this was so true about today. Maybe fortune cookies do turn out to be accurate," Rohit remarked excitedly. "Gautam, why don't you pick one for yourself? Maybe it will give you some clue about the way forward."

"Nah, I don't believe in all this. Let's go," Gautam replied and proceeded to exit the restaurant. However, unseen to Rohit, Gautam had already picked up a fortune cookie and slid it into his pocket while Rohit was reading his. He was definitely not going to open it in front of Rohit, though, to get some smart-ass comments.

As they came out of the restaurant, Rohit put an arm around Gautam.

"Hey, I forgot, you still have to answer two of my questions."

"Which ones now?" asked Gautam in a tired and disgruntled voice.

"Have you slept with her yet and is she still a virgin?"

Gautam's smile was back as he saw the mischievous grin on Rohit's face.

"Dude, you are sick," shouted Gautam, as he chased Rohit down the road to give him a whack.

GAUTAM HAD SET UP THE MEETING WITH HIS ELDER sister, Richa, a day earlier. He wanted to pass his decision through her as he had done for all important moments of his life. Even though they had an age gap of six years, Richa was more of a friend to Gautam, and he treasured and valued her immensely. Both of Gautam's parents were working during his childhood days, and it was Richa who would take care of her dear brother – be it with his studies, his homework or even just by playing with him.

One of the lasting memories of his childhood that made his bond with Richa even more special was the day she took him to the hospital with a deep cut on his right arm. He was ten years old then and had tripped and fallen while trying to catch the ball, playing cricket with his friends in the building compound. The chain of the cycle he had fallen on had cut through his arm, leaving a deep gash. Richa was home alone but managed to take Gautam who was howling in excruciating pain, to the doctor.

She single-handedly picked him up and ran down the road until she could find a taxi, and then carried him into the hospital. She bravely got Gautam to calm down, be his support, and finally got him stitched up by the doctor. He could never forget that day and knew that his sister would always be there for him, whatever be the situation.

The day she got married was the day Gautam cried the most. As she was leaving the marriage hall, bidding adieu to the entire family, Gautam could not control the tears that he had been holding back for the previous twenty-four hours. For five minutes, he hugged her and cried like a baby. No words were spoken between them, but the feeling of separation was leaving a big void in Gautam's life. Though she was moving only eighteen kilometres from him, he knew things would never be the same. She was moving on to a new life. A new family.

One thing she had taught Gautam while growing up was a value for time, which had made him distinctly punctual, in most cases arriving before time. He knew reaching late would mean getting an earful from her. After leaving Rohit, Gautam took an auto rickshaw in order to reach Linking Road, Bandra. He was racing against time, as the traffic meant he was surely going to be late. He cursed Rohit all the way during his ride, knowing that, had it not been for his long-drawn lecture, he would have been on time.

After marriage, Richa had moved to Vashi, part of the planned city of Navi Mumbai which was a satellite town of Mumbai. She had come down to Bandra to shop on Linking Road, a street lined with the most well-known designer brands as well as cheap, good quality clothes on the streets at amazing bargains. She was preparing for a wedding in her husband's family and was running short of time.

Gautam got off the auto for the last stretch of two hundred meters as the road was badly jammed and made a dash to their meeting place.

He reached outside Starbucks, trying to figure out where his sister was sitting when he heard a familiar voice. "Hey, Gautam, your pretty sister is over here."

Gautam saw Richa sitting at one end of the coffee shop, sipping a cappuccino, with Gautam's favourite frappe already lying on the table. Even after having a child, Richa had maintained herself nicely, thanks to the umpteen sessions of yoga.

Gautam joined his elder sister and, after a quick hug, sat down adjacent to her. "You are looking really beautiful today," remarked Gautam with a pleasant smile.

"Little brother, don't try to butter me up. Just tell me what trouble you are in now. Did you again accidentally kill another of dad's pet dogs?" joked Richa. She was referring to an innocent incident that had happened more than ten years ago, when Gautam threw his dog's treasured ball out of the window in order to tease him, as he was irritated with its continuous barking. The dog jumped after it. The rest, as they say, is history.

"Sister, I am bored of killing dogs. I think I want to start with humans and you are the person I'd like to start with!" Both of them burst out laughing, just like the good old days.

Gautam knew time was short, as he had to return to the office and his sister was also on a tight schedule. So, without beating around the bush, he took out the small box from his pocket and offered it to Richa.

"Please open it," he requested.

There was an immediate smile on Richa's face when she opened the jewellery box. The glittering diamond ring took Richa by surprise and made her a tad emotional.

"Awwww... You should not have done this for me, little brother. You are simply the best!"

"My dear sis, this diamond ring is not for you, sorry," responded Gautam with a smirk on his face while snatching the ring back. "The large diamond that your husband gave you, does that not suffice?"

"You do realise that diamonds are a woman's best friend," retorted Richa, after which the realisation dawned on her, and she put her hands on her face excitedly. "Oh my god, my brother is about to propose to his girlfriend! Wow! This is big news, but why did you not tell me that you had a girlfriend? Did you want me to meet her here? But if you just want me to meet her, then you would not have brought the ring here. Oh my god, you are going to propose to her in front of me!" Richa was bubbling with excitement, as she blabbered away.

Gautam shook his head in dismay. "Sis, you talk too much. Can you just hear me out? If that is even possible. Please."

Richa apologised and calmed down so that Gautam could explain himself.

"You know, Richa, I can't make any major decision in my life without your consent, and hence I have come to you to ask for advice," Gautam said in a dead serious tone. "I love this woman but I think mom and dad will have a problem, and that's why I need your support and understanding."

"Why? Is she deaf, dumb or blind? Come on, Gautam, no way are they going to object. Our parents are extremely chilled.

In fact, they will heave a sigh of relief that a girl actually likes you," smiled Richa. "On a serious note, bro, they accepted my love marriage six years ago. I don't see why they will object to yours now."

Gautam took hold of Richa's left hand and explained to her, slowly and in a low voice, "There is an age difference of twelve years between Roshni and me."

Richa pulled her hand back as she broke out into a hysterical laughter. "Child marriage is illegal, bro. You want to marry a thirteen-year-old girl? You sicko! Forget our parents, even the police will have an objection to that!"

Gautam was not laughing. He had a dead serious look on his face and was annoyed at his sister's hysterics. "I am the younger one in this relationship. She is thirty-seven years old."

"What?" shrieked Richa at the top of her voice. "Are you crazy?"

Everyone at Starbucks stared at them, as Richa put her hand up in apology for her loud tenor.

"Listen, Richa," whispered Gautam. "I thought you would understand my situation, which is why I am talking to you. I don't want you to react like our parents may. Just hear me out."

Gautam was a bit nervous, but he was prepared with what he had to say to his elder sister. "First, to clarify your doubts, she is not a divorcee. She has been single till now. When she was twenty-three, she lost her parents in a bad train accident and thereafter she has lived alone, working long hours making ends meet because of her parents' debts. She was so career-driven that she never found the time to get married," said Gautam with utmost sincerity, which showed his love towards Roshni.

"So where did you two meet?" asked a composed Richa, reverting to her understanding self.

"Roshni is my senior in the office. I was working on a group project where she was our head trainer and we were reporting to her for approximately a month," Gautam started narrating to Richa how he fell in love.

"When I saw her for the first time, I was totally knocked off my feet. She looked so beautiful like a girl I always dreamt about. At that time, though, I did not know about her personal life or her marital status. I was simply amazed by her style of working, her smartness, her frank attitude and, above all, her simplicity. To be honest, after seeing her day in and day out for a month, I developed a crush on her. Though the truth is that I, too, never saw any future in it especially since she was my senior." Gautam was being very candid about his initial introduction to Roshni.

"After our project was over, I did not see her for a couple weeks. One day, I was in a restaurant with some of my building friends, when I noticed her sitting alone. So like a thorough gentleman, I went to greet her."

Gautam went on to explain to Richa, in detail about what had transpired thereon.

Three and a half months ago

GAUTAM HAD BEEN SITTING IN THE RESTAURANT FOR around fifteen minutes before he noticed Roshni out of the corner of his eye, sitting all alone. He had come with a few friends from his locality for just a round of starters, as they had planned to go clubbing later. However, noticing Roshni sitting alone, he excused himself, informing his friends that he needed to give company to his boss to remain in her good books and for future growth in the company. The friends grudgingly agreed but asked him to join them later for drinks. Gautam, however, was hoping to spend as much time as possible with his crush.

"Good evening, Miss Roshni. If you don't mind, may I sit with you," requested Gautam humbly and in a distinctly charming way.

Even though Roshni was thirty-seven years old, she did not look her age at all. In fact, she could have easily passed as someone in her late twenties. Her dark brown hair was relatively short, going only till her shoulders, and she preferred to keep it clipped for a more formal look. However, that night, she had let it loose and looked stunning. She kept herself fit with a regular eight kilometre walk.

Walking and listening to Bollywood music was a practice she had developed soon after her parents' death to keep herself occupied and her mind diverted. Being a single child, she had always been close to her parents, and their death had caused her grief to no end. Her last meeting with them at the train station would play in her mind endlessly – a memory that she never wished to erase.

Roshni had a very humble background, with her father working as an ordinary clerk in a big national bank and her mother, a teacher. To fund Roshni's MBA, her father decided to opt for the voluntary retirement scheme so that the bulk money he received as compensation could be used to manage things. All his savings went into her education, while her mother's salary funded their daily expenses.

Her parents' death had turned her into an independent woman overnight. She immersed herself in office work to avoid going home and being alone. Her perseverance, determination and hard work were what had pushed her up the ladder to the post of Senior Vice President in one of the world's largest multinational banks – no mean achievement for a single woman with no family support. It was also her father's dream that she would make it to a senior position in the corporate sector, which she had been chasing ever since the completion of her MBA course.

Taking up specialised projects like analyzing clients for mergers and acquisitions was her forte. It was during one of these projects that she had come across Gautam. Among a group of nine people, Gautam easily stood out. His tall frame, along with a well-built body, silky hair and good looks were enough to classify him as handsome. But to add to his looks, he was also sincere, reputed for working hard and intelligently, studying problems and finding solutions. All of this made him a standout performer in the team – a fact that made Roshni fond of Gautam.

So when she saw Gautam greeting her after a break of a few weeks, she was pleasantly surprised and glad that he had come forward to meet her.

"Oh hi, Gautam! How are you doing? Please do have a seat," she invited him with a big smile. Roshni looked beautiful in a long, embroidered white kurti, which she wore over a pair of dark blue jeans.

They were in the lively restaurant of Punjab Grill, known for its exquisite North Indian cuisine, located in the Mumbai suburb of Lower Parel. It was Gautam's favourite restaurant, the menu of which he had memorised. To add to it, the restaurant management also offered him a unique loyalty discount.

"Why is a beautiful woman like you sitting all alone in a restaurant? I tell you, Ms Roshni, we men just stop caring about our wives after we are married," remarked Gautam in a slightly flirtatious way. He had heard some office gossip that Roshni was single, but he just wanted to make sure so that he would not make a fool of himself.

"First of all, Gautam, you can call me Roshni here. And secondly, I am not married. I am just waiting for my aunt," replied Roshni in a frank tone.

Gautam was pleasantly surprised and repeated the line Roshni used but slowly, with a big smile and a shake of his head. "You are not married."

Gautam, ever since the project was completed, had not been able to stop thinking of her. He was in complete awe, not just for her beauty but also for her intelligence. Though, he also knew that he could do nothing about it, as she was his senior in the bank.

However, the opportunity at the restaurant had come out of the blue and Gautam did not want to let go of it.

Gautam, beaming after hearing the news, asked Roshni, "So, does a junior colleague like me stand a chance?"

Roshni took a moment, before responding with a slow dismissive shake of her head. "Can we slow this down, Gautam? You seem to be in a flirtatious mood. Did you just break up with your girlfriend?"

Before Gautam could reply, Roshni's mobile rang and after a brief conversation, she hung up the phone. She gestured the waiter to come to their table.

"Gautam, what will you have for dinner?" asked Roshni casually.

Gautam was pleasantly surprised with the turn of events. He had bargained to spend a few minutes with Roshni, but now he was about to have dinner with her. What luck!

"So, Roshni, you really want to have dinner with me? Cool," said Gautam with a mischievous smile as he took the seat opposite her.

Roshni flashed a wry smile as if to acknowledge that it was not the most prudent decision. "Don't read too much into it.

My aunt who was supposed to join me had something come up all of a sudden and can't make it. Plus, I just hate having dinner all alone. It is especially embarrassing and boring."

Gautam volunteered to order his favourite dishes since it was Roshni's first time at the restaurant. They were served curd kebabs and tandoori broccoli for appetizers, followed by spinach with cottage cheese, black lentil, and tandoori naan for the main course.

While the food kept coming, Roshni and Gautam remained locked deep in conversation, barely taking their eyes off each other. Various topics were discussed, especially about Gautam and his years growing up, his college days and his entry into Global Bank.

"You know, Roshni, my getting into the bank was a matter of luck. At our campus interview in NMIMS, I had already been selected by a big telecom company based in Mumbai. But my best friend, Rohit, had an interview lined up for the bank and he forced me to accompany him.

However, they would not let me enter the room without filling in the application, which I eventually did after much persuasion from Rohit. You see, I never held the banking industry in high esteem. I failed to understand them. They would never lend money to the people who needed it, and they would chase after the people who did not need money, to lend it to them."

Gautam went on with his interesting narration. "And the same thing happened at the interview, though I came off better in the exchange." Gautam chuckled and continued, "Rohit was desperate to get into the bank because of his dad's background, though he never wanted to use his father's clout and instead was trying to make a career on his own terms. The interview board liked him and confirmed his employment, but with a salary package that was not as per Rohit's expectations. He, though unwillingly, accepted it. During my turn, they were again impressed and offered me the job, which I flatly refused, informing them that I was joining a telecom company. I don't know what they whispered among themselves, but they told me that they would give me thirty percent more than the package I was offered by the telecom giant. From then on, I swear I love the bank and the banking industry." Gautam burst out laughing.

Two hours had flown by since Gautam had sat at the table and the dinner was nearly over. Roshni felt extremely comfortable in Gautam's company though she still could not open out to him about her tragic past. She had kept her emotional shield up but knew that if they continued to meet and talk like this, she would eventually give in. Roshni felt a genuine connection with him that she had never experienced before.

"To top it off, we shall now have the special betel-leaf mint shot," announced Gautam, gesturing to the waiter and clasping his hands in glee.

They took their shots, then ordered another round and gulped that down too with great delight.

Roshni had a good time and volunteered to pay the check since she had invited Gautam. He reluctantly agreed to let her pick up the tab.

As Gautam's friends had already left the restaurant, Roshni volunteered to drop him home, and this time, there was no reluctance, but silent elation on Gautam's part.

Gautam was quickly falling in love with Roshni especially since he now knew that she was single and fun to be with. He had an enjoyable time with her and the connection was something he too had never experienced with any woman before. He did not want this to be their last meeting and was desperate to find a way to meet her again.

While Roshni was driving the car towards Gautam's residence in Prabhadevi, which was just a short drive from Lower Parel, he was silently wondering how to trick her into going out with him again.

The car came to a halt below Gautam's building and he finally broke the silence. "I don't know about you, Roshni, but I really enjoyed your company," said Gautam, as he removed his seatbelt to get down from the car.

"You know, Gautam, I also happen to like my own company – another coincidence," quipped Roshni on a lighter note.

They both smiled. It was time to part and neither knew how to end it. There was a bit of awkwardness, to say the least.

Gautam mustered up some courage and asked, "So, by any chance, is your aunt again going to stand you up this Saturday night? If she is planning to, then maybe Indigo Deli in Bandra would be a good place to do it. What do you think?" Gautam was looking Roshni in the eye, hoping for an answer in the affirmative, his fingers crossed in anxiety.

"I am getting late, so could you excuse me, Gautam?" replied Roshni in a cold voice.

Gautam was crestfallen and was numbed by Roshni's refusal. His hopes had been dashed. Maybe it was just him who had felt the connection. Without saying a further word, he opened the door of the white Toyota Altis and put his foot out. Roshni realised Gautam's feelings had been hurt but she wasn't sure whether to pursue this relationship or not.

"My aunt eats early, so I will be waiting for her at eight in the restaurant." Those words subconsciously came out of Roshni, surprising her too.

They shared an awkward handshake and then she took off as well. Gautam was a little dazed and could not believe what had just happened. Roshni had agreed to meet him again.

As Gautam ended the narration, he and Richa had also finished their drinks and requested for the table to be cleared. Gautam continued, "I went back home that night, and the smile never left my face until I met Rohit today to discuss this relationship. The last three months that we have been seeing each other have been the best of my life."

RICHA VOLUNTEERED TO DROP GAUTAM TO HIS OFFICE, as it was on her way back. She had to return home soon as she had left her two-year-old son, Aarav, with her mother-in-law. Once they were comfortably seated inside her chauffeur-driven car, Richa asked Gautam, "So what do you like about her?"

Gautam was always honest and open with his sister. "Everything. There is not a single thing that I dislike about her. She is a complete woman. She is independent, capable of making individual decisions, abundantly smart and intelligent. She is also witty with an amazing sense of humour and spoils me by cooking amazing food; at the same time she is exceedingly understanding and highly knowledgeable because of her vast experience. Roshni is a truly beautiful woman, in every sense of the word, not only physically but more importantly, in terms of her nature. All in all, she is the complete package.

She is what I have always dreamt of in the woman I wanted to marry and spend my entire life with. In my eyes, she is just another twenty-five-year-old girl. For me, her age has never been a factor and frankly speaking, I have never even noticed it," concluded Gautam, trying to make Richa see his perspective.

Richa took her brother's hand and gave it a reassuring squeeze. "The way you describe it, I want to meet Roshni right now," she said very earnestly with a broad smile.

"You know, Rohit had actually called before you reached and informed me that you would be late because of him. He also told me about Roshni and that you might actually be in love. He was, in fact, feeling remorseful that he challenged your love. So I wanted to hear your side of the story and exactly how you felt about Roshni. I think it is wonderful that you feel so strongly about her. But the things Rohit brought up, they are worth pondering."

"So all this time you knew about Roshni and said nothing?" Gautam appeared upset.

"Yes, but like I said, I did not want you to preempt your feelings while opening up to me – the things you related, your love for Roshni, your emotions, your intense feelings about her. I am sure you would have skipped those if we were to only focus on her age. Yes, age is a big factor, but it is not the only consideration here. What Rohit did not tell me, though, is that you were going to propose to her with the ring. That was a surprise to me."

Gautam hugged his sister tightly, appreciating her thoughtfulness and patience to hear his feelings. "You are the best, sister. I love you so much."

"I am not done yet. I feel I need to advise you on a thing or two," Richa told Gautam softly but firmly. "You need to realise that this is not America, where it is acceptable for a marriage to last only five to seven years. Divorce is a big social taboo in India and after that, finding a woman again is exceptionally difficult unless you happen to be a celebrity. So you need to tread carefully. Now is the only time you can think. Once you get married, it's for keeps. No looking back, no lingering doubts."

"But Richa, if one were to get a divorce due to any kind of incompatibility or misunderstandings then it can occur even when the couple is of similar age. It has become overly common even in India now," said Gautam defensively. "I can't get into a marriage thinking it's going to end in a divorce, can I?"

"That's true, Gautam, and that's why I am counselling you that now is the time to think. You can't afterwards, once the decision is made. A divorce may or may not happen, but in your case, there is a higher probability. Just because of the age gap, the chance of differences coming up is much higher. It's just like how your probability of getting hit by a car is greater when you are walking on the road as opposed to when you are walking on the pavement. You are the only person who can decide the pros and cons, my brother," said Richa, putting the ball back in Gautam's court with a gentle pat on his back.

"I can't decide on your behalf and tell you what is right or wrong. There comes a time in life when you need to make a decision on your own and stand by it. Please don't take the easy route of letting others make the decision for you. But, little brother, whatever decision you make, I will be right behind you with all the support you need from me."

The car stopped across the road from Gautam's office building, and both of them stepped out to bid adieu. Richa gave Gautam a tight hug. "I love you so much, brother, and cannot believe how fast you have grown up. Take care and don't worry."

As Gautam was about to cross the road, Richa called out to him. "One more thing. I was just lying earlier when I said that Rohit was remorseful. He was actually laughing his guts out." The siblings smiled at each other and had a chuckle, trying to make light of Gautam's difficult situation.

Gautam went back to the office, but his mind was no longer at work. He could not concentrate on anything and looked a bit jaded. The events of the day, first the proposal to Ms Bregenza, then the game of truth and dare with Rohit, and finally the emotionally draining discussion with his sister, had left him dazed. He left the office a few hours earlier than his usual time and headed home. He wanted to be alone with his thoughts.

Gautam reached his house in Prabhadevi a vastly confused man. He resided with his parents in a three-bedroom apartment on the fifth floor of a relatively new building, which had ample car parking space and a small garden for children. Luckily, his parents were not at home when he reached, saving himself the need to justify his being home early. The entire way back from his office, all he could think about were the various scenarios that Rohit had discussed with him.

For Gautam, his room was heaven, where he could be by himself in solitude. He had personally taken charge of the decoration. Going against the general norm of painting the walls, he chose to wallpaper his room. The accent wall behind the bed had a New York–styled skyline wallpaper in a copper brown combination, with the other walls being done up with beige and white broad stripes to give a brighter feel to the room. He had a small study at one end of the room with a small collection of management books and a tan brown reclining chair next to his bed which was the ideal place to sink into to watch television. For him, his bedroom was the cosiest place in the whole world – he could just be himself there.

But on that day, even his room was unable to soothe him. He was no longer sure about proposing to Roshni and marrying her. He faced himself in the mirror, trying to propose to her with the same conviction that he had practiced the night before. He tried once, twice… five times, but he just couldn't do it. Suddenly, the desire had gone.

To lighten up his dour mood and view his relationship with Roshni in a positive light once again, Gautam started recollecting the happy moments that they had shared together. Their last date just couple of days earlier was still fresh in his memory.

It was Sunday evening, which they had decided to spend together watching a movie in Roshni's apartment in Juhu. Roshni had cooked dinner at home making Gautam's favourite corn spinach. The oscar award winning movie *Gravity* had just ended with Gautam heaving a big sigh of relief.

"Wasn't that such an amazing movie about human emotions? What one can accomplish with one's back against the wall situation, is truly astonishing," Roshni summed up the movie, gently caressing Gautam's hand which she had held tightly for the entirety of the movie. "What did you think?"

"I thought you were looking damn cute and pretty during the movie. I just could not take my eyes off you. In my opinion your side profile is killer," Gautam was at his wooing best. He was pleased that the movie was finally over and he could converse with his lady love.

As Gautam leaned towards Roshni to kiss her, she smiled mischievously, turned her head in the opposite direction, slowly let go of his hand and proceeded towards the kitchen to get dinner ready. Gautam grinned and followed her to the kitchen to lay the table.

"You know Roshni, I am so lucky to have spent so much time with you. Time has just flown by and it's already been three months since we started dating. This has probably been the best phase of my life. When I saw you for the first time in our office, I thought to myself, how lucky your husband would be to have a woman like you in his life. Then, I got the opportunity to work under you for the project and ended up developing such a big crush. But I have to confess, I always feared speaking to you. I thought you were the serious types and a strict follower of rules." Gautam was all smiles looking at Roshni as she brought out the delicious looking food from the kitchen.

"You are not the first one to tell me about my aloof nature," said Roshni with a slight shrug of her shoulders as she sat down on the dining chair. "I know, it has been three wonderful months and I have truly enjoyed my time with you, Gautam. Something which I did not expect, to tell you the truth. However tell me honestly, what are we exactly doing here? Is this just a fling for you?"

Roshni had never been in a relationship with any man. She had shown the world her stern and serious persona as a shield towards the advances of various men she had come across throughout her career, wanting to concentrate only on her work. Gautam was the first person with whom she had let her guard down and been herself. She did not want her relationship to be based only on sexual attraction and had thus avoided any physical relation with Gautam. For both, it was their first serious romantic bond.

There was a period of silence as Gautam gathered his thoughts on a question which he was not expecting that night. He took Roshni's hand in his, "I had a huge infatuation on you and kept wondering how my life would be with you in it. Three months down the line, I have the answer to it. I have been in love with you from the day one and just feel blessed to be around you. For me, being with you, spending time with you, is the most important thing which gives me a high in life. I of course find you hot and sexy but my love towards you is far beyond that."

It was the first time that Gautam had confessed his love to Roshni. He had kept his feelings to himself till then, not knowing whether it would be reciprocated by her or whether it was too early in the relationship to let out his emotions. However having declared his feelings, he felt a sense of relief and elation.

Roshni leaned towards Gautam and placed her hand on the side of his face. There was a moment where both of them looked at each other with nothing but love filled in their eyes. Gautam's heart was pounding as their lips locked together for their first kiss.

"Does she really love me as much as I think she does? She did not say I love you back to me that night." Gautam reminisced his date which was the turning point in their relationship. He had realised then, that to convince Roshni about the seriousness of his feelings and his commitment to her, it was important that he propose to her sooner than later.

"But whatever Rohit said makes sense," he thought aloud. "That's why I did not want to say anything to him in the first place. He has completely ruined my feelings. Love is not supposed to be practical. That's why it's the heart which falls in love and not the brain," the frustration blurted out of Gautam.

At the time when Gautam was trying to make sense of the situation, his phone rang. It was Roshni calling. This was the last thing he wanted at that point in time. Talking to her then would have felt like cheating on her. Gautam was never good at hiding his emotions.

"What should I say to her? I cannot talk to her in this state of mind. Please hang up, Roshni, please hang up," he pleaded to the phone.

The ringing stopped, and he heaved a sigh of relief.

After a brief silence, it started ringing again. Gautam held his head in despair and looked towards the sky for divine help. He hesitantly picked up the phone, having no idea what to say.

"Hi Gautam. Where are you? You have not replied to a single message of mine today. You were not even picking up the phone. I did not see you in the office today, either. Are you okay? I was all worried and anxious to hear your voice. I hope everything is good." Roshni sounded hugely worried.

"No, no, I am good. I was just a bit preoccupied the entire day. I am so sorry," Gautam apologised a bit nervously, as he was lying to Roshni, something which he never wanted to do in his life.

"I am so glad to hear your voice. I was really concerned. I couldn't even concentrate on work today. Not being able to talk to you did something weird to me…" Roshni tapered off with a nervous laugh and continued, "Anyway, where are you taking me for dinner tomorrow?"

Gautam had totally forgotten that he had planned a dinner with Roshni and even made reservations at the Taj Land's End, a premium five-star hotel bang on the sea in Bandra. It was the perfect location to propose to Roshni, or so he'd thought. But since he had become unsure about the whole thing, he had to continue with his lie. "I have not decided yet. Can I let you know tomorrow, please?" Gautam replied sheepishly.

Roshni could sense the tension in his tone. "Yesterday you said that there was something important to discuss. What is the matter?" she queried gently, trying to calm Gautam down.

"Is it about your one-year foreign placement training? Do you want to discuss that? I know that you have said no, but do you wish to talk over your decision with me?"

The one-year international placement was important to further one's career. It would be a launching pad for senior management in the bank and Gautam had been handpicked by Global Bank's director for the great potential he had seen in him. At the same time, Gautam had also taken internal tests and cleared them with flying colours to deserve a seat in this privileged lot.

Rohit, his best buddy, was also part of this group. However, a week earlier, Gautam had informed the director of his inability to go for the training, citing family issues. His real reason, though, was actually he did not wish to be away from Roshni for such a long time. He had fallen so much in love and was so habituated to being with Roshni that he could not imagine spending a whole year without her.

Roshni – who, along with the director, Alok Nanda, was in charge of the selection process – had a long chat with Gautam regarding his refusal to go. She had reasoned with him that it was the best move for his career but to no avail. He had continued to cite his family reasons for not wanting to go – parents being too old, him being emotional about leaving them and so on. Gautam did not want to tell her the truth, as he wanted to surprise her with the proposal and catch her off guard.

However, now he was no longer confident about this choice. He suddenly felt like he had too many crucial life decisions to make at the same time. He definitely could not propose to Roshni in such a state of mind and had to make an excuse for cancelling the dinner date.

"I am not sure about tomorrow's dinner, Rosh," replied Gautam in a low, guilty voice. "Some of my cousins from Delhi are here, so I will be busy tomorrow evening. Can I call you later? I was with them only right now and in the middle of something," Gautam added to his bundle of lies and hung up hurriedly.

He had lost his appetite and ate very little for dinner. After a quick shower, he hit the bed, hoping that a good night's sleep would help ease his tension and make him think clearly. However, the moment he closed his eyes, weird thoughts and scenarios about Roshni from his conversations with Rohit and Richa kept coming up. He kept tossing and turning in his bed. He was about to have an emotional breakdown. It seemed that the future he had all figured out was turning into a mirage.

Finally, out of sheer mental exhaustion, he fell asleep at four in the morning with the lights still on.

HIS MOTHER'S PERSISTENT KNOCKING ON THE DOOR finally woke Gautam up.

"It is already nine. Are you feeling okay? Don't you want to go to the office today?" Gautam's mother shouted at the top of her voice. Gautam realised he was already late for the important foreign assignment meeting in the office. A quick glance at his phone showed five missed calls from Rohit, Payal and his other colleagues who had been selected for the one-year programme. Even though Gautam was the top achiever in the group, Payal was the deserving second while Rohit had come in third.

He quickly got dressed after a shower, the entire time cursing himself for the delay on an extremely important day. He picked up his packed breakfast, ran out the door and climbed into the lift. His taxi was already waiting for him outside the building. The office was a good thirty-minute drive from his home. In the rush of leaving his house, he did not get time to think about what he was finally going to do about either Roshni or his international assignment. Somewhere, he knew that both the decisions were related.

If he wanted to marry Roshni, then ideally he should not go for the assignment, and stick to the plan decided earlier. Long-distance relationships never tend to work. However, if he wished to get away from Roshni and be by himself, then it was best to go abroad for a year. He was in the taxi alone and knew time was running out for him. Just as he was about to pull out his phone from the pocket of his trousers, the fortune cookie from the Chinese restaurant fell out.

He thought to himself, "Looks like god is trying to tell me something through this. Maybe whatever is written on it will give me a clue about what to do."

Gautam could not decide anything till then and thought this was the only way to hopefully take the right decision. After a long thought and a deep breath, he broke open the cookie and unfolded the chit, which read, "It's better to be alone sometimes." Gautam threw his head back in despair, knowing that it was not the kind of message he wanted his fate to deliver. Even the Chinese seemed to be against his love.

Gautam reached the office an hour late and rushed on to his floor. The second floor was where the operations department was stationed, handling the entire administration work of the bank, networking across all its branches and offices. It was the nerve centre for keeping the bank's operations flowing smoothly. Thus, no lethargic attitude from any employee was tolerated.

Rohit, with a sandwich in his hand, was standing at Gautam's desk to greet him. "Hey, bro, you look sick and exhausted today. What happened? Are you all right? Who did this to you?" asked Rohit in a mischievous tone, looking at Gautam's crappy dressing.

Gautam was usually dressed smartly, but on that day, half his shirt was hanging out, his trousers were wrinkled as he was wearing the same pair he had the day earlier without ironing them. In the extreme rush, he had even forgotten to comb his hair.

"You, Rohit! You!" Gautam pointed his finger at Rohit threateningly. "You screwed with my mind, and this is the outcome. I should have never come to you to talk about my personal issue. What a blunder on my side to have trusted a joker – a womaniser like you."

"Did you break up with her?" asked a nonchalant Rohit while munching on his sandwich, oblivious to Gautam's threat.

"No, I did not break up with her, but I broke my head thinking about her. And now I feel like breaking your head." Gautam's anger was mounting with every passing second.

He moved towards Rohit with menace and came face to face with him. They were barely millimetres away from each other, with Gautam's six-feet plus frame bearing down on the slightly smaller five-feet, nine-inch body of Rohit. It seemed that the best friends were about to trade blows.

Rohit, in order to defuse the tension between them, playfully licked his lips. "Do you want to smooch here or should we go to the men's room?" he said in a serious tone, all the time looking into his buddy's angry eyes.

Gautam's feisty stare gave way to a sheepish smile as he backed off. It seemed everyone else in the office had started ignoring the antics of the best friends and they went about their work as if nothing was happening.

"Anyway, our meeting about the foreign placement is rescheduled. It's in an hour in the training room," informed

Rohit. "It got postponed because of your late arrival. I am just hoping we both get placed in the same city. Hopefully Singapore. What an amazing time we will have then! Best buds together." Rohit hung out his hand to deliver a high five to Gautam who in turn deliberately ignored it. Gautam was not in an excited or celebratory mood as his best friend.

Rohit was unaware that Gautam had already said no to the placement a week before.

"Yes, let's see," replied a pensive Gautam, still undecided whether to take the foreign placement or not. Gautam snatched the half-eaten sandwich from Rohit as he was still hungry and walked away towards the restroom to get spruced up.

An hour later, all the nine selected individuals for the foreign placement, along with Roshni, assembled in the training room. Her senior, Mr Alok Nanda, Director Pan India Operations, was chairing the meeting. The training room which could accommodate about forty people at one time, was set up like a classroom with a large whiteboard at one end which could be used for writing as well as double up as a screen for the projector to relay digital presentations. Before Mr Alok Nanda could begin, Gautam apologised to him and everyone in the room for his late coming due to which the meeting had to be rescheduled.

Mr Nanda acknowledged Gautam's apology and started with his address to the selected group. "I am highly delighted with the progress all of you have made in the past year. So now is the time to reap the benefits of your hard work and go for the one-year international placement. I cannot stress enough, the importance of this move for your career. You will get a global experience of how everything works on a level far higher than what you have worked on so far."

Every person in the room was feeling proud of his or her own achievements and the fact that he or she had been selected amongst hundreds of fellow employees who had applied for this management training.

Mr Nanda who was standing and facing the group in the training room announced, "Everyone in this room deserves a big round of applause." There was a thunderous round of clapping. Even Gautam managed to feel proud of his accomplishment.

Once the cheering stopped, the Director continued, "I have one more bit of amazing news to share with all of you. If you do exceedingly well in your profile, then the Asia headquarters in Singapore is where you will get your permanent posting."

Everyone was stunned with this information. They were all under the impression that, like the previous years, they would have to come back to India after a year. But now, to get placed abroad was the chance of a lifetime.

"Rohit, stop grinning," scowled Alok Nanda. "If you thought this was going to be the fun part of your training, then get over it. Each of you will be working for himself or herself, as the case may be, putting in a minimum of twelve hours a day without holidays. You will not even get the chance to come to India for a break." However, Mr Nanda's description of a tough worklife couldn't dampen the excitement everyone felt about the prospect of working abroad for a year.

Alok Nanda continued, "Before I announce the allocation of cities, I need to clarify something. I am a little disappointed, Gautam, that you have chosen to remain in Mumbai for some reason. As I have just explained, a foreign placement is very important for furthering one's career."

Everyone, including Rohit and Payal, was shocked about Gautam's choice. They could not think of any reason why he would come so close to a management position and then let it go. Roshni, on the other hand, had a sparkle in her eyes. Even though he had given Roshni the excuse of family issues, she knew that he had not told her the truth and her gut feeling was that it was their relationship that was keeping him from going. Remaining in Mumbai would mean spending more time by her side, which gave her immense satisfaction. However, more pleasing for her was the fact that Gautam was willing to sacrifice so much to be with her. A gesture of true love, she thought to herself.

Gautam had deliberately positioned himself in the training room to sit behind Roshni in the same row so that he could avoid eye contact with her at all times. He wasn't bold enough to look into her eyes and tell her what kind of turbulence was going through his mind.

"But Gautam, considering your exceptionally good record, and the fact that you were the highest scorer I am willing to give you one more chance. Do you want to stay here or move ahead?" asked a hopeful Mr Nanda.

After a deep thought, with a few seconds ticking away in pin-drop silence, Gautam, his fingers still dwindling with nervousness replied in the affirmative. "I think I will move ahead, sir."

"Are you sure?" asked an elated Director Nanda, who had personally mentored the team and wanted all of them to be successful.

"Should we lock it?" Alok Nanda tried his best to imitate Amitabh Bachchan, the Bollywood icon and the host of the Indian version of 'Who wants to be a Millionaire.'

"Yes, sir," replied Gautam with a slow nod.

"Great!" Nanda clasped his hands in delight.

Everyone was beaming and smiling, but Roshni was shocked at the sudden turn of events, and sadness enveloped her face. "Why did Gautam unexpectedly change his decision? Does he not want to be with me anymore? Is this the gesture which clarifies that his career is more important than our relationship? Why did he not even bother discussing such an important decision with me? Why just cut me off?" Roshni was suddenly tormented with all these questions with Gautam's unexpected change of stance.

"Since you have decided to go, Gautam, you and Payal get Singapore. Rohit, unfortunately, you now have to shift from your earlier allocation of Singapore to Seoul, South Korea," announced Alok Nanda.

"What? Korea? But sir, I am a vegetarian. And there, they even eat dogs! Nobody from India visits that country. In fact, that country never even promotes tourism," pleaded Rohit profusely, coming out with all kinds of reasons he could think of, but to no avail.

"The decision has been made, Rohit. Believe me; it is a fun place to be, especially for a single guy like you. In fact, I would like to term it as the Paris of Asia," Nanda responded to Rohit with a wink. "I am circulating this paper for the rest of you to know where your respective placements are. Everyone will leave together in one week. All the best, people. Do us proud," he wished them and left the room after congratulatory handshakes with all the candidates.

Gautam glanced at Rohit with a grin. Rohit, on the other hand, was fuming.

Gautam shook his head and with a big smile prophesied, "Karma, my friend, karma. It has come back to bite you in your ass. And that too, big time."

For a moment, Rohit's situation had made Gautam forget his own issues.

As everyone congratulated Gautam and welcomed him back into the programme, Roshni left the room in a hurry, without even glancing at him. She was tremendously disappointed and did not know how to react. Walking out, rather than facing Gautam, was the best option, she felt.

It now made complete sense why he had been ignoring her for the past day. For her, the biggest sense of hurt was the fact that he hadn't discussed anything with her. Just when she had opened herself up emotionally for the first time to someone after her parents' death, she felt betrayed.

Was this the end of their love story?

GAUTAM BECAME EXTREMELY NERVOUS, NOTICING Roshni's behaviour. It was on expected lines, he thought to himself, especially if she felt let down or betrayed by his actions –or, for that matter, inactions. He remained all alone in the training room, while the rest had left excitedly to inform their family and colleagues. Rohit had gone after Alok Nanda to persuade him to assign his profile to any place else apart from South Korea. Gautam seemed to be the only person feeling unhappy about the foreign placement. But that was the situation he unfortunately found himself in.

"Should I go and speak to Roshni?," he pondered. "Or is she so upset with me that in a fit of anger, she will be rude or even slap me in front of everyone?" Gautam knew he was wrong in the way he had handled the situation. He made Roshni believe they had a future together and then, out of the blue and without even discussing it with her, he made a decision which may have effectively ended their relationship.

He started imagining what could happen if he approached her. She could be raging mad, give him a mouthful of the choicest of bad words and literally kick him out of the office.

Not only would this spoil his image in the office, but it would also put a question mark over his future in the company. Everyone would come to know about their affair, and that could become a blot on both their characters. Office romances, especially with seniors, were always looked upon suspiciously as stepping stones to growth in the company.

After a lot of thought, he finally decided it would be prudent not to approach Roshni in the office, but maybe call her after a couple of days, giving her time to cool down and let the whole thing sink in.

Over the weekend, he wanted to call her on several occasions, but every time he just could not muster enough courage to do that. He knew that the situation was his doing which made him hugely embarrassed and guilt-ridden about calling her. It was his first breakup and he was unable to handle the awkwardness associated with it. The entire weekend was spent thinking about the situation and what Roshni would be going through, but he still did not show enough guts to call her. Finally to delay the eventual conversation, he selfishly decided that it would be wiser for him to wait for Roshni's call.

"Maybe she needs time to think this through, and at an opportune time, she'll call me," he thought to himself.

There was less than a week left for Gautam to leave, and he had a lot to do. He needed to pack a lot of stuff. His shopping list was exhaustive and time was limited. He and the rest of his colleagues who were to go abroad were excused from routine office work. They had to report back only for the handover within their respective teams. This was a blessing in disguise for Gautam, for one, he could finish his shopping and preparations for the trip in time and, more importantly, he could avoid meeting or seeing Roshni in the office, thus avoiding the embarrassment of a face-to-face meeting.

Gautam could complete most of the handover over email from his home, but the day before he left, he was called into the office to sign off his reports and bid adieu to everyone. More importantly, he needed to hand over all the physical documents and his ID card, among other things. While getting into the office, he was nervous as hell with his stomach wildly churning, hoping and praying not to bump into Roshni.

However, as fate would have it, exactly the opposite was in store for him that day. His entry into the office was followed by a sequence of embarrassing events.

While walking towards his desk, where Rohit was waiting for him, he saw Roshni coming from the opposite direction. Gautam did not know what to do or how to greet her, so he chickened out brilliantly by suddenly changing directions and going left towards the men's restroom. He waited there for five minutes before slightly opening the door to peep outside and ensure that Roshni was not in sight. Gautam reached his desk and sat down, a bit relieved over the close call. He knew he had to finish things quickly and leave. Even when Rohit tried to get his attention, Gautam was indifferent, as he wanted to finish his pending work as soon as possible.

As Gautam was about to complete the reports on his desk, he saw out of the corner of his eye, Roshni coming towards his cubicle. His desk was next to the passage that led to the other side of the floor which Roshni had passed an hour earlier.

He suddenly turned towards Rohit and pulled his chair right next to him, trying to show that he was engrossed in a serious discussion and hence could not notice anything or anyone around. Gautam and Rohit spent a few minutes animatedly talking about a few football issues as they both loved the sport and passionately followed their respective clubs. Gautam was a diehard Arsenal fan, whereas Rohit was a bleed-blue Chelsea follower.

Gautam started off with a smirk on his face. "I hope you have given up the EPL title dream after being savaged by my team, three goals to none. Arsenal blew Chelsea away in the match. Chelsea had absolutely no response to my team's creativity and guile. You can't say, though, that the result was out of the blue. It would be an irony in itself, given that Chelsea is called The Blues." He let out a wicked laugh. "You just wait and watch, this year Arsenal is going win the English Premier League for sure."

Rohit, being Rohit, was never the one to accept defeat, just like Chelsea. He shot back, "Win the EPL title? You must be joking! They won the last title fourteen years ago. I was just eleven, living in Delhi, had not tasted alcohol and had never even traveled to Mumbai. I am ready to bet anything on them not winning the title this year. As far as Chelsea is concerned, this was the wakeup call they needed. Losing against Arsenal is like hitting rock bottom. They can only rise from here."

Gautam could not bear hearing Rohit any further and stood up to look around for any sign of Roshni. She was long gone. He heaved a sigh of relief and went back to his cubicle, leaving Rohit hanging as the conversation had not yet ended.

Rohit knew something was wrong, seeing Gautam's weird behaviour since the time he had entered the office.

He asked his best friend nonchalantly, "So what is it with you and Roshni nowadays? You seem to be avoiding her like crazy. What is the matter? Did you guys have a fight?"

Gautam was shocked. "Is it so noticeable?" he queried anxiously.

"There was so much tension when you both were around in the training room last week that I could have cut it with a knife," replied Rohit.

"Listen, however much you might want me to share my personal problems with you, I am not encouraged to do so. So let's not discuss this. I think I am capable of making the right decisions without you messing up my mind," said an irritated Gautam.

"So, you leaving Roshni… is it the right decision?" asked Rohit casually without batting an eyelid.

"What do you mean?" a perplexed Gautam counter queried. He could not believe that Rohit was now questioning his decision to leave Roshni, especially given that it was he who had polluted his mind in the first place.

Rohit continued, "I thought you were made for each other. You looked picture-perfect together. Add to this the fact, that you were so comfortable in each other's company – the age gap being rendered completely irrelevant. The questions, I posed were just to make you aware of the various scenarios that were probably ahead of you. I certainly never suggested for you to break up with her."

Rohit saw his friend's face turn red with anger in response to his reply and felt it was best to leave before the situation got out of hand again. "Anyways, I have to go. I am done with my work and handover formalities. See you at the airport." Rohit hurriedly said bye to his colleagues and left the building.

Gautam shook his head in disgust at Rohit's response. How could his best friend confuse him like this? One day, he was against the relationship, and now he was for it. How could Rohit do this to him?

Gautam sank in his chair, pondering over Rohit's words. He thought to himself, "Be strong. If I have decided on something, let's stick to it and not let the mind waiver. Whatever happens, happens for the best. I have decided to be without Roshni. So be it. No looking back now."

Gautam finished the rest of his work and quickly said his goodbyes to colleagues and left the premises, not knowing whether he would settle down in Singapore permanently and ever return.

Gautam, Rohit, and all their colleagues were leaving together on Saturday afternoon by Jet Airways. While Gautam and Payal's final destination was Singapore, others were transiting the city and thereafter catching their connecting flights, to Seoul and Manila, among other cities.

Gautam was all dressed and packed for his trip to Singapore. Whenever he travelled, it was customary for him to visit the Prabhadevi Temple to worship the goddess after whom the area where he had lived his whole life was named. Gautam was a religious person with a firm belief in god. He believed in fate and knew that one good act always came back to you by karma in double the kindness, but so did a bad act. That day though, he had also gone to the temple to beg forgiveness for hurting Roshni and breaking her trust.

Soon after, he was back home, ready to leave. He was hoping that Roshni would call him, so he could speak to her one last time before he left. That's where the law of attraction – the belief that, by focusing on positive or negative thoughts, a person brings positive or negative experiences into their life – helped Gautam. Just when he was picking up his bags to leave for the airport, he got a call from Roshni. He excused himself from his parents and went back to his room to speak with her privately.

"Hi, Roshni," he said gingerly with a touch of nervousness.

"All the best for your trip and do well. I was calling everyone from the programme, so how could I miss my favourite of them all?" said Roshni, with a touch of sadness in her voice.

Gautam was engulfed in the pain he had caused Roshni. He knew he had made a big blunder and not owned up to it. He was overpowered by the feeling of guilt.

"Roshni, I am extremely sorry for not being able to communicate with you for the past week. I wanted to talk to you so much but I just couldn't. I have not been myself lately. I am so sorry." Gautam could hardly hold his tears back.

"Please, Gautam, don't be sorry. You have not done anything wrong. Getting the opportunity of settling down in Singapore had to be your first priority. I completely understand that. I just feel bad that you were not upfront enough to let me know your feelings. I hope, one day you will grow up and realise that. Anyways, all the best and do well. Bye." Roshni hung up before Gautam could register that she was crying.

It had been an extremely tough week for her emotionally, but her maturity made her conscious of the fact that the age difference between them might have finally caught up with Gautam. He would have ignored it in the beginning, but the realisation must have eventually dawned on him. Crying in front of Gautam would have weakened him. She did not want him to have second thoughts about leaving for Singapore and furthering his career. That would have been selfish on her part.

Gautam took his parents' blessings by touching their feet, and left in the waiting cab. Once Gautam was alone in the taxi, he finally let go of his emotions and cried profusely. He knew he had done an extraordinarily inconsiderate and insensitive thing by leaving Roshni high and dry. Finally, his emotions got the better of him, and he sobbed the entire way to the airport.

Gautam left Mumbai, his mind in complete turmoil, hoping to start a new chapter in his life in a better and positive way.

A MONTH HAD PASSED SINCE GAUTAM'S ARRIVAL IN Singapore. He tried to keep himself occupied as far as possible, so as to keep his thoughts off Roshni. He was putting in long hours in the office, working twelve hours a day and even on the weekends. For him, being alone at home was an emotional torture; being left alone with his thoughts just brought back memories which he wanted to block. It was as if the beautiful city of Singapore did not exist for him at all.

Payal, on the other hand, was enjoying her experience of working in a new city. Even though she was matching Gautam's work timings during weekdays, weekends were fun, especially exploring the lively and happening city. Singapore is a melting pot of various cultures, with Chinese, Indians, Malaysians, Europeans and Americans among others calling it their home. It had become a regional business centre for Asian operations of various multinational companies, especially after Hong Kong being taken over by China from the British in the nineties.

The world viewed the Chinese takeover with suspicion, given its communist background, and hence many organisations preferred moving to Singapore, with the added incentive of the income tax rate being as low as ten percent. Singapore was home to a vibrant corporate culture, especially the banking industry, with swanky buildings lining the Manhattan-style skyline and brilliant infrastructure provided by the highly proactive government. Of course, being surrounded by the Pacific and Indian oceans added to the glamour quotient of this colourful city.

Gautam and Payal were provided separate accommodations by the bank within the same local area, and they were quite happy with the arrangements. The first month had been distinctly hectic for them. At the end of it, they were to give a joint presentation to Global Bank's senior management in Singapore on their recommendations for better risk management of cash deliveries and deposits in the developing countries of Asia, including India, Thailand, Malaysia and the Philippines. For the research on this topic, they had to go through a voluminous amount of data across countries before analyzing, streamlining and then forming opinions on them. It was a Herculean task, and what made it even more difficult was that their recommendations were to be presented to the head of operations in Asia and his core team. Both Gautam and Payal however were aware that success in this project would go a long way in getting them permanent postings in Singapore.

It was the night before the presentation with Gautam and Payal working extremely hard to ensure that they meet the deadline. It was 11 p.m. in Singapore with the skyscrapers looking even more brilliant with their sparkling lights switched on, while the calm sea had ships lined up at the harbour. This was the beautiful view from Payal's apartment on the sixteenth floor, which both she and Gautam were oblivious to, due to the work at hand.

Payal was seated at the dining table with her laptop, while Gautam was furiously working on his Macbook on the couch. The place was a mess, with sheets of paper lying all over. To save time, they had even decided to skip going to the office that day and work from Payal's house. In the one month of working together, they had struck a great rapport and the partnership was working extremely well, each knowing the other's strengths.

While Payal was an expert in analyzing data, Gautam's forte lay in finding solutions to problems brought up by the data. They had developed a good comfort level with each other. Gautam had consciously tried to keep his relationship with Payal strictly professional. He was not in a state of mind for socialising and partying, still carrying the guilt from his breakup with Roshni. Payal had tried her best to get Gautam to move out and enjoy the city, but he had steered clear of all her requests.

"Payal, I think we are going to meet tomorrow's deadline. Wheew!" Gautam said in a highly relieved tone with his eyes still pinned to the laptop. "Until yesterday, I was not sure that we would finish this on time. But you are something, Payal."

He pointed at Payal enthusiastically and got up from the sofa to walk towards her. "Could never have done this with any other partner," he concluded while patting her on the back. It was genuine appreciation from Gautam for the effort Payal had put in.

Payal was blushing. She always had a soft spot for Gautam and being in Singapore together, away from their families, had made them spend a lot of time with each other. Hearing such loving words from Gautam only added to her feelings towards him. She had a crush on Gautam since their Mumbai days, but working with him so closely and in a city far away from home was making her fall in love with him.

"It's teamwork, Gautam," Payal replied with a big smile pasted on her pretty face. "We are partners, and our lives will be incomplete without each other."

While Payal was replying, Gautam was looking for soda inside the fridge with the door open. What he heard from Payal startled him, and he was unsure whether he had caught the words correctly. He looked back at Payal, who still had a smile on her face. On seeing Gautam's expression, she snapped out of her daze and realised what she had just uttered.

"What I meant," she stutteringly clarified, "is that the project would have been incomplete without each other."

She was relieved when Gautam bought her cover-up and picked up the soda from the fridge.

Just as Gautam opened the can to take a sip of the chilled cola, his mobile rang. He was glad to see that it was his sister, Richa, calling. She had been extremely busy with the wedding in her husband's family and had been unable to take out the time to talk to him at length since he had landed in Singapore. Gautam excused himself and went into the kitchen to receive the call.

After the initial greetings, his sister asked the obvious. "So how have you been holding up? You okay now with the decision of not going ahead with Roshni?"

Before he boarded the flight to Singapore, Gautam had spoken to Richa from Mumbai airport and informed her about his painful decision of breaking up with Roshni.

"Sis, it is nearly a month since I came to Singapore and despite the tight schedule, not a single day has passed since I have not thought about her. I see her everywhere – in the office, on the streets, in my apartment. I can't seem to get her out of my system. I am just trying to block the memories from my mind by keeping busy, but it just does not seem to be working," Gautam replied in a particularly sober voice.

"My dear brother," replied Richa, "you just need to ease up a bit. I know you are an overly emotional person, but sometimes you need to just let go of things. Maybe you should try liking some other girl, and that will automatically wipe out this memory. I am sure there are a lot of beautiful women in Singapore to fall in love with. Have you tried?" Richa was concerned for her younger brother and tried to make light of the situation.

"I wish it was that simple," replied Gautam in a soft, frustrated tone. "Your solution for getting out of love by falling in love with someone else is the worst advice I have ever heard in my life. What is more worrying is that it is coming from my elder sister, whose advice I value the most." It was now Gautam's turn to engage in a little banter of his own.

Richa found herself in a spot and the firing line. She quickly decided to change the topic with the first thing that came to her head. "So where are you now?"

Gautam hesitated a bit before replying, "I am outside for some office work."

He was hesitant whether he should tell Richa the truth that he was at Payal's apartment. She was sure to misunderstand the situation and definitely try to make a big deal out of it.

At that very moment, Payal, who had not seen Gautam for a while, called out for him loudly. He had no option but to respond to her, or else Payal would have continued shouting out his name. He rolled his eyes and knew he was caught in a fix, as Richa would have definitely heard a girl's voice in the background.

"Who was that?" asked an inquisitive Richa, smelling something fishy.

Gautam could never lie to his sister.

He responded with the truth, "That's Payal. I am at her place for work. We have a huge presentation tomorrow in the office, and we were just finishing that." He was a touch embarrassed, not knowing what Richa would make of it.

"Isn't she the same girl who went with you from the Mumbai office? She is so beautiful and smart. I am just checking her profile on Facebook. Looks fab! Maybe she is the one, Gautam. Remember, fate has brought you together in Singapore at an opportune time. Just go for her, bro." Richa was brimming with excitement with the sudden turn of events.

"Thanks for the advice, Richa. I will surely consider it," said Gautam in a sarcastic voice and quickly hung up, knowing too well that continuing the conversation would not be in his best interests.

Gautam took a deep breath, trying to collect his thoughts, and went back to the living room, where they had been working all day. The Macbook was switched back on again, and he resumed his task of giving the finishing touches to the presentation.

Richa's recommendation about Payal started to hit him, and he began thinking about it. His concentration was suddenly hampered, and he started to steal glimpses of her. Payal was casually dressed in a purple t-shirt and blue jeans with her long dark hair loosely tied at the back, but she still managed to look her pretty self. Gautam thought to himself, "Payal is indeed, immensely attractive, smart, hard-working and fun to be with. Should I be thinking of her in some other way? She could be an ideal partner. Is she the one? Are destiny and god bringing us together?" Gautam's thoughts were all over the place and the unveiling of their pitch to the management team was no longer his focus.

Gautam reminded himself of the presentation's importance for his career and forced himself back to concentrating on completing it. After a few minutes of furiously working on the computer, he looked up at Payal, but this time he could see Roshni instead. He shook his head, trying to refocus, and looked again to see if it was Roshni or Payal. But now, he could only see the face of Roshni.

"Earlier, it was Rohit, and now my own sister has corrupted my mind," muttered Gautam in frustration. "Why can't my supposed well-wishers just leave me alone?" His focus was gone, and he decided it was best that he left and let Payal finish the final piece herself.

"Listen, Payal, I am suddenly not feeling too good," said Gautam, while rising up from the couch and pointing embarrassingly towards his stomach. "Could you just put in the finishing touches alone, please?"

Payal looked at Gautam, who was now sporting an unusually irritated look, wanting to just run away from the apartment.

"If you have an upset tummy, you can use my toilet. It's okay with me," remarked Payal innocently.

Gautam burst out into nervous laughter with a slightly embarrassed look. "It's not that. I can shit practically anywhere – even this room would do. But I want to spare your home the foul smell and keep my impression intact."

He went to Payal and gave her the customary hug. "Thanks a lot for everything. It has been an amazing day."

But as he was hugging her, his thoughts drifted to Roshni, and for a minute, he thought that he was holding Roshni in his arms, instead of Payal.

The words "I love you so much" subconsciously came out from him.

He immediately realised his mistake and came face to face with Payal,

"I owe you – I owe you so much for this," he nervously repeated the words and rushed out before he could commit another mistake. He ran towards the lift as fast as he could without even bothering to look back.

Gautam, however, failed to perceive Payal's feelings. She was still standing at the door, already very much in love with him.

GAUTAM CAME BACK HOME, FRIGHTENED BY HIS OWN emotions. He had made a hurried exit from Payal's apartment to escape his feelings about Roshni. To concentrate on his work and avoid all things that reminded him of her was all that he wanted. Gautam had an early morning presentation and could not afford to be late for it. He forced himself to sleep by thinking about his childhood days, which he spent holidaying with his family. His vacations included trips to the beautiful hill stations of Mahabaleshwar and Lonavala, the beach destinations of Goa and Kerala and the historic locations of Rajasthan and Delhi.

He fondly remembered his grandparents, with whom he used to spend a few weeks every year during summer in their hometown of Ludhiana, the largest city in the state of Punjab. They would always take him and Richa to one of the famous religious places in the north of the country. The visits to Chintpurni Temple, Vaishno Devi, Badrinath, Yamunotri, Haridwar and Rishikesh, amongst others, had opened him to his spiritual side. He was eternally grateful to his grandparents for this enlightenment.

Gautam had a good night's sleep after nearly a month and was grateful to his parents and grandparents for the wonderful childhood they had blessed him with. He was back to his old, perky and happy self, which boded well for the important day ahead. Gautam was confident that, along with Payal, he would make a great impression on the senior management with their crisp presentation that could perhaps, if implemented, save millions of dollars for the bank.

A couple of hours later, a big round of applause went up in the conference room of their modern and chic office, on the completion of the near-perfect presentation of their project. It was a crowd of around twenty-five people, with the country heads of treasury operations from almost all Southeast Asian countries present. Included in the crowd was Mr Shim, the Asian Head of Treasury Operations and the person whom Payal and Gautam hoped to impress the most.

Everyone present in the conference room took turns congratulating both Payal and Gautam. Coincidentally they had dressed in the same colour. Gautam was looking smart in his three-button grey suit with self-embossed pinstripes, a light pink shirt and a grey tie to match, while Payal looked ravishing in a grey pencil dress.

As they were together, taking in all the accolades from the various delegates, Payal excused herself to receive a call on her phone.

While Payal was away, Mr Shim came forward to acknowledge the great research work done by them. "Nice presentation, both of you," Mr Shim congratulated Gautam in his Korean accent. "You both make an exceedingly good pair.

Keep up the good work. The content was to the mark with no deviation from the topic. The observations and points you brought up are worth debating and implementing in order to have big cost savings for the bank. After the lunch break, I am meeting all the country heads again, and these points are going to be a big part of the discussion. Well done once again. Please hand over the presentation to my assistant to take it further."

"Both of you have a great future together in the bank. Very well done," appreciated Mrs Helen Lewis, Corporate Affairs Director, as she left the conference room with Mr Shim.

Everyone had left the room after congratulating them, with only Gautam and Payal remaining behind. Gautam was feeling a sense of immense pride with what they had achieved, as well as a little embarrassed about the accolades his team work with Payal had received. They had perfectly rehearsed their presentation, intertwining their talk and thereby impressing everyone with their coordination.

Gautam was all packed up and ready to leave, before realising that, for the last fifteen minutes or so, Payal had been continuously speaking on the phone. Noticing her talk with so much enthusiasm, an alluring smile to go with, while looking so beautiful at the same time, Gautam found himself getting attracted to her.

As soon as her phone call was over, Gautam walked towards her.

"Come on Payal; it is not only you who gave an amazing presentation. I was a part of it too, remember? So how come you are getting so many calls of appreciation and I am not?" asked a puzzled Gautam, pointing to her phone.

"I don't know, Gautam. Maybe, because it is my birthday today and some people, unlike you, do remember it," replied Payal with a wry smile on her angelic face.

Gautam was flushed red with embarrassment. He could not believe that he had forgotten her birthday, especially after the memorable celebration the previous year, when she had taken a few of her colleagues, including him, to party in Hard Rock Cafe at Worli. Everyone was extremely high that night and Gautam, the only sober one, had to drop the majority of them home. It was also the night that Payal had started developing a soft spot and a liking for Gautam. His discipline about not drinking alcohol since he was driving, despite peer pressure, in addition to his selfless act of ensuring that everyone reached home safely made him a kind of hero in her eyes.

"I am so sorry, Payal. So, so sorry. Not only for today but for last night as well. If I had known it was your birthday, I would have definitely stayed back and we could have brought it in together. Wish you a very happy birthday and may god bless you with the best of everything," said an apologetic Gautam, while giving her a big bear hug. "Listen, I think I can make this up to you. What say we take rest of the day off and go sightseeing, shopping, watch a movie and then have dinner to rejoice this beautiful day? All on me."

The happiness and elation of the highly appreciated presentation had snapped him out of the rut he was caught in. Payal's birthday provided the right opportunity for him to go out and enjoy the city of Singapore. It also gave him a chance to show his gratefulness to Payal for her great support.

"Gautam, it's a great plan, but you don't need to do this as an apology," replied Payal with a smile. "I have already forgiven you. Don't worry."

"No, I need to do this. I owe you one, remember?" said a determined Gautam. "I am actually pretty excited to spend the day outside of the office with you. I have just been locked inside four walls for the past month."

Payal agreed with enthusiasm, especially looking at Gautam's excited expression. She was personally overjoyed with the prospect of spending her birthday in his company. This also presented her an opportunity to get to know Gautam more intimately outside work and get a feel for his thoughts about her.

It was a great day in Singapore. Pleasantly warm with clear blue skies. After a month's hard work, they finally got to enjoy the city together. The first stop on their day out was the Universal Studios theme park, which was packed with a lineup of stunning rides, spread over forty-nine acres of land.

However, before going there, Gautam insisted they head over to Orchard Road, the longest shopping street in Singapore, lined with some of the biggest malls in Asia. Every brand worth its name was present, be it the high-end Louis Vuitton, the Spanish brand Zara or the British brand Superdry. They quickly bought new casual clothes from Zara, both of them slipped into blue denims and smart T-shirts. Gautam footed the bill as promised, which Payal reluctantly let him.

They entered Universal Studios with Top of the Line passes, which gave them direct access to all rides without having to wait in the long queues. Adrenaline was flowing with each and every roller coaster they rode, including the Battlestar Galactica, which was the highlight of the park. Every ride and every show, including the live performance of the *Waterworld* movie was exciting and fun. It took them nearly three hours to explore the entire park.

They left the theme park after having a quick bite and decided to try an adventure sport– something more physical, since they were just sitting during the majority of the rides. They picked out a place called Forest Adventure as it resembled a set of the famous MTV India reality show *Roadies,* which both Gautam and Payal watched. It was as if they were going to be a part of the show, with more than thirty obstacles to tackle – climbing trees, hanging on ropes, Tarzan-swinging from one tree to the other and finally zip lining over the lake. It took them a couple of hours to finish and by the end of it, they were both overjoyed but extremely tired.

It was already late in the evening, nearing seven o'clock, and Payal wanted to go home and rest after the highly eventful day. However, Gautam insisted they should have dinner together to round off the amazing day. He had a great time with Payal, doing things he loved. Gautam had always been an outdoor person, although he had become exactly the opposite for the past month. Roshni was far from his thoughts at that moment.

Gautam suggested taking Payal to a place which he had heard great reviews about. It was the Equinox restaurant, perched on the seventy-third floor of the luxury five-star property, Swissotel. It overlooked the harbour and probably had the best view in the city. Being there at dusk with the sun just setting was an ideal thing to do. The restaurant was renowned for its modern European cuisine along with local Singaporean dishes.

Gautam had already made the reservations during the day to avoid being turned away from this popular restaurant. Payal was extremely excited about the dinner, thinking Equinox would serve to be the ideal place to start a new romance. Payal and Gautam stepped inside the restaurant, and their jaws dropped, looking at the beautiful sight in front of them. The sea, the harbour, the skyscrapers – the entire city looked serene from up there. A postcard photo of the sight was permanently etched in their memories.

They were seated next to the tall French windows with a breathtaking view in front of them. Payal had a twinkle in her eyes. She could not believe that her day was turning out to be so perfect. Gautam had taken care of her very graciously and probably picked the best place in Singapore for her birthday dinner. "How thoughtful he has been the entire day towards me. Maybe he has similar feelings for me," Payal thought to herself.

"So what can I serve the young couple?" asked the waiter designated to their table. He was in his mid-forties and dressed in a gold vest and black trousers.

"Oh we are not a couple, just good friends and we are celebrating her birthday today," replied Gautam with a nervous laugh.

"I apologise, sir, it was just that both of you are wearing similar clothes which couples do, and you look so cute together," said the waiter with a smile.

"Point noted," said Gautam blushing, and he proceeded to order the drinks and food. They ordered a couple salads, fries and pasta to go along with their cocktails.

"The waiter does have a point; we do make a cute couple," said Gautam in a naughty and flirtatious way. He had no idea that his words were making Payal more certain about his feelings for her.

They spent the next couple hours talking about each other's personal lives, their growing-up years and their families. They shared their aspirations and ambitions with each other.

Payal came from a well-to-do family, with her father being a prominent architect. Her mother was an interior designer, and both had met and fallen in love when they worked as juniors in a highly reputed architectural firm in Mumbai. After marriage, her father started his own practice, with her mom playing a supporting role. The firm had done decently well and given good repute and income to the family.

However, Payal – the only child to her parents – never had any inclination towards designing. She instead chose management studies, which had brought her to the very same bank where Gautam worked. Both had joined the bank around the same time, which had made them develop a good working relationship over the years.

"So, Gautam, how many girls have you gone out with?" asked Payal staring into his eyes. She wanted to gather as much information as she could about his personal life.

"To tell you the truth, no one so far. I tried many times but still no luck. Hope that does not make me sound like a loser," replied Gautam in jest. He was apprehensive about telling Payal of his relation with Roshni.

"It was an office romance, so it would be better to keep silent about it, especially with fellow colleagues," he thought to himself.

"What about you, Payal? Guys must have always been swarming around you," Gautam reversed the question.

Payal was very open and frank. "They did, actually, but I did not see a future with any of them. You know, I did not believe in the mushy idea of falling in love. You need to be emotionally mature to know and understand each other, which I believe you are not at a young age. Plus, I did not want to be stuck with a guy who has no clue what he wants to do in life besides falling in love."

"So have you become emotionally mature enough to fall in love now?" asked Gautam, persisting about her thoughts on love.

"I guess I have, and I feel like giving it a trial run," replied Payal with a mischievous smile.

"Oh really?" Gautam looked her in the eye, which gave Payal goose bumps. "Waiter, can you please come here?"

Payal was in a state of shock and turned white in fear. She shrieked, "What are you doing, Gautam? I meant a trial with–"

Before she could finish her sentence, Gautam cut her off. "Check, please," he told the waiter with a big grin on his face.

As soon as the waiter left the table, Gautam broke into a big round of laughter. "Look at your face! But you look even more stunning when you are angry." Payal threw the salt shaker at Gautam, disgusted by his silly joke.

The waiter brought out a small round chocolate cake with a candle on top and 'Happy Birthday Payal' written on it. Gautam had placed the order for it when he had earlier excused himself to go to the restroom. Photos of the two good friends were taken by the waiter while cutting the cake, as a couple musicians serenaded Payal with a birthday song. Payal could not believe what was happening and was overcome with emotions, thinking about the entire day and how Gautam had gone out of his way to make it perfect for her.

Gautam willingly settled the check, and they left the restaurant.

The two of them decided to take a walk across the famous Clarke Quay, a historical riverside promenade that is lined with the best restaurants and clubs in the city – the centre of the vibrant nightlife of Singapore.

As they began their walk parallel to the river and away from the crowd, Payal took Gautam's hand in her hand and tilted her head to rest on his arm. They walked silently, with the cool breeze blowing across their faces.

Gautam felt a shiver. Was he falling in love with Payal, just as his sister thought and wanted him to? He put his arm around her waist and continued walking, with neither saying anything. They were caught up in the moment.

Payal, on the other hand, had no doubts about how Gautam felt for her. All his actions of the entire day screamed out his love towards her. She was already in love with him, and her guess was that it was the same with him.

The road ended by the sea and they stopped in front of the white Merlion monument – the national symbol of Singapore. It was a very beautiful and romantic place, with the famous opera theatre in the shape of a beaver in the background, alongside some of the tallest buildings in the world, located in the commercial district of Singapore.

"I hope you had a great birthday and I made up for my memory loss," said Gautam in an apologetic but loving voice.

Payal hugged him tightly. For a minute, there was a pin-drop silence. Payal was stopping herself from crying, not out of sadness but out of sheer joy.

"This was the best birthday of my life. Thank you for everything," said an emotional Payal as she pulled herself back and looked at Gautam with nothing but love in her eyes.

She moved forward, Gautam responded, and they kissed passionately without any inhibitions. It was a picture-perfect moment for the young couple and all it needed was the beautiful Bollywood song '*Kuch Kuch Hota Hai*', playing in the background.

As they were kissing with their eyes closed, Gautam suddenly saw an image of him kissing Roshni and became even more delighted. The memories of being with Roshni started rushing back to him. But then, images of the day he had spent with Payal hit him and the realisation dawned on him that he was kissing Payal and not Roshni.

He immediately backed away and appeared panic stricken, feeling as if he had committed a crime and cheated on Roshni.

"What happened?" asked a perplexed Payal, surprised at the sudden turn of events.

"This is weird, Payal – you and me," replied Gautam in a guilt-ridden voice.

"It is not, Gautam. I am in love with you, and I don't feel weird at all. In fact, I am jumping with joy inside," replied Payal honestly.

"Listen, Payal, there are some issues in my head that I need to clear, that I can only do so by being alone. I hope you will understand," pleaded Gautam, requesting Payal's patience. It was the second time in two days that he was leaving Payal stranded high and dry. Payal had no clue what was happening to Gautam on the inside.

Gautam's eyes welled up as he started to leave.

"Take your time, Gautam. But remember, I will be waiting for you," replied Payal with tears rolling down her cheeks.

GAUTAM WAS BRIMMING WITH CONFIDENCE, SPORTING a big smile, which clearly suggested he was madly in love. To complete this perfect picture, he was holding a ring for his lady love. A ring in one hand and a bunch of roses in the other, he knocked on the door in a calm and self-assured way, adjusting his blue checkered shirt and smooth hair. He had to look impeccable when making the proposal.

This was the moment he had been waiting for. The moment he proposed to the woman of his dreams.

The door opened slowly. Gautam immediately bent down on his knee.

"I am extremely sorry for my previous behaviour. I do not know why I did that. I beg for your forgiveness and understanding." Gautam seemed very sincere in his appeal. "Now, I have made up my mind, and I am going to do what I should have done a long time ago." Gautam paused, opened the ring case and continued, "I love you from the bottom of my heart and would love to spend the rest of my life with you."

Gautam took a nervous, deep breath, readying himself for the final appeal. "So, Ms Roshni, will you marry me?"

Roshni had her hands covering her mouth the entire time during Gautam's proposal. She could hardly breathe in excitement at seeing Gautam after more than a month. And, on top of that, he was on her doorstep on a Sunday morning, completely out of the blue and unannounced. If that was not enough, he was on his knees, proposing to her. The anguish, the pain and the sullenness of the last month had suddenly evaporated, and there was only happiness written all over her fair and pretty face.

She too knelt down, facing Gautam with tears of joy rolling down her pink cheeks. "Yes, I love you so much. You don't know how much happiness you have brought to my life today. But you have to promise, that you will never leave me again."

Roshni and Gautam hugged each other while crying profusely at the same time. The emotions of separation had hit them hard. In fact, it had made them both realise their deep love for each other.

"I have so much to say to you, Roshni. Only god can now separate me from you. Nothing else matters to me but you." Gautam was a relieved man and was overjoyed that the emotional rollercoaster of the last month was finally over and Roshni, the love of his life, was in his arms.

Gautam held her hand to put on the ring, which fitted perfectly. Roshni absolutely loved it. As they got up to enter her apartment, Roshni asked the last question Gautam wanted to hear at that time. "Gautam, have you thought this decision through? I hope you are aware that you will be marrying a woman twelve years older than you."

Gautam gave her a wry smile. "There is nothing in this world that I have thought of more, and I could not be surer than what I am today."

Gautam looked into Roshni's eyes and reassured her, "You are perfect for me."

They both entered Roshni's two-bedroom apartment in the plush area of Juhu, where many famous Bollywood stars reside. Her house was decorated in a traditional way, with her passion for paintings clearly visible. The furniture was basic and made of teak wood in dark brown polish; there was nothing flashy about it. All the walls were off-white, with a different set of paintings hanging on each wall. In the living room, there was a small wooden swing for two, where Roshni would spend most of her time at home. As they say, the house is representative of one's outlook and attitude. Roshni, too, was a down to earth person and a simpleton at heart.

"Gautam, you need to tell me what exactly happened before you left for Singapore. I was stunned by your complete lack of communication and then the sudden decision to go for the international placement." Roshni wanted everything honestly clarified before they entered their new phase.

Gautam wanted to start with a clean slate too and did not want to hide anything from Roshni about what had transpired. He went on to explain to her how Rohit had seeded doubts in his mind by recreating various future scenarios that could happen between them, which would ultimately lead to a breakup or divorce. His sister, Richa, had been supportive of whatever he decided but requested him to put proper thought into the decision-making process, rather than do things hastily and repent later.

"All of these things combined together to put serious doubts in my mind about our relationship, and I wanted to get away from it all. I desperately wanted to speak to you, but I thought that discussing age gap issues may hurt you deeply, especially given that you had been so open with me. I was also scared about what all of this could mean to us working together in the same office. I guess I just chickened out and ran away to Singapore." Gautam had love and sincerity written all over his face, about which Roshni had absolutely no doubt.

"Okay, I get all of this, but what happened in Singapore that made you come back so quickly, within only five to six weeks of leaving Mumbai? I thought that you guys were not allowed any long breaks on this assignment. Are you back for good?" asked Roshni probingly.

Gautam was in a fix. How much should he tell her about Payal and what had happened between them? Should he skip a few details to avoid the uncomfortable questions from Roshni? But in the end, he decided it would be prudent to be completely honest with her and if there were consequences, then so be it.

Gautam related to her his month in Singapore and how he had worked and worked to avoid dealing with his emotions about her. The one good thing that happened, though, during this phase was the successful presentation that he and Payal had given, which was highly appreciated by everyone across the Asian region and especially the director, Mr Shim.

"The same day, earlier this week, something else also happened, which made me realise how deep my love is for you and how I can't think of spending my life without you," Gautam recollected his time.

He explained to her in detail what had transpired between him and Payal, including the kiss. "It was at that point when I knew and I was sure about how much I love you. The kiss with Payal made me feel guilty, as though I had cheated on you," said Gautam very honestly and hung his head in shame waiting for an outburst from Roshni.

"In that case, the person I need to thank for bringing you back into my life is Payal," responded Roshni with a forgiving smile on her face. "Had it not been for her, you would have still been in Singapore, sulking, and me mirroring your emotions in Mumbai. I hope, though, that you will not kiss her anytime in the future," she quipped and elbowed Gautam in a playful way.

"Of course not, ma'am," Gautam responded and hugged her tight. "You are so cool, Roshni. I was bracing for a backlash from you, but you proved me wrong."

"Honesty is the best policy, Gautam, and as long as we keep it that way, we will never have any issues in our life," Roshni replied. "But what about your one-year assignment in Singapore, then?"

"That was the tricky part. I met Mr Shim, who was kind enough to spare some time for me. I explained my situation, and he reluctantly agreed to post me back in Mumbai, although with a couple of conditions," replied Gautam, trying to build some kind of suspense.

Roshni, who was jumping for joy at the prospect of Gautam being relocated to Mumbai, became curious about the terms. "What are those?"

Gautam continued, "One is that I have to operate out of the Nariman Point office and the second is I have to work according to Singapore time, which is two and a half hours ahead of India. This means I have to be in the office by 7 a.m. What a bummer! I may also have to occasionally fly to Singapore for work and will be reporting only to my Singapore boss."

Roshni was clearly impressed with the deal Gautam had made with Mr Shim, who was known to be a no-nonsense guy. "Wow, they have really bent their policies for you, Gautam. They must be saving millions of dollars with the suggestions you made in the presentation. I am so proud of you."

Gautam was basking in the glory of his achievement and the bargain he had struck with Mr Shim. It had taken him two hours and the staunch backing of his immediate boss in Singapore to get this done. Moreover, the bank wanted to be flexible with an employee of such high caliber and performance.

Then came the question from Roshni that brought him back to earth. "I hope you informed Payal about your decision and have let her know about our relationship. I am assuming you did not leave her hanging, the way you did with me." Roshni appeared serious in her tone, as she did not want another girl to go through the same anguish and agony that she had dealt with.

"I know, I know. I learnt my lesson. I could not make the same mistake twice. I did go to her place the next day and apologised for leading her on."

Gautam proceeded to tell Roshni what had transpired between him and Payal at her apartment in Singapore.

For Gautam, the entire day after the presentation went by in convincing his bosses to let him relocate back to Mumbai.

On the way back from office he decided to meet Payal to pour his heart out and tell her the truth about his relationship with Roshni.

"I have come here to apologise for my actions. I was not thinking with a clear mind and inadvertently led you in believing that I had romantic feelings for you," Gautam confessed as soon he was seated in Payal's apartment.

Payal was surprised, especially considering the passion that Gautam had displayed the previous day. "Are you trying to tell me that the entire day – the dinner, the kiss everything was a mistake? An error of judgment?"

"I was trying to get over a relationship that I felt had ended. In fact, I was the one who had ended it. I was not honest with you when you asked me yesterday whether I was ever in a romantic liaison and I replied in the negative. It was not that I wanted to lie to you, but my relationship was such that it would have been better if you did not know. Moreover, I had no idea whether you and me would end up being a couple." Gautam was trying extremely hard to explain his state of mind to Payal.

Payal, however, was still in a state of shock. Gautam was the last person she had expected to lie to her. However, given the fondness she had harboured for him all these years, she wanted to hear him out before jumping to conclusions.

"So what are you exactly trying to tell me, Gautam? You had a secret romance that you can't share me with me? How am I supposed to understand anything you say, then?"

Gautam knew that hiding important details was not the ideal way of expressing regret. He continued his explanation.

"I was in a relationship with Roshni. The reason I had to stop kissing you was that I am still in love with her. Even when I kissed you, I thought for a moment that I was kissing her. Kissing you felt to me like I was being unfaithful to her. That's why I was so scared. I ended my relationship with Roshni as I thought that a lot of issues could crop up in our lives in the future due to the age difference between us. I had felt it would be better to quit now, rather than repent later."

Payal was stunned. "You and Ms Roshni? I can't believe this. Though I do understand now why you did not want to tell me about her earlier. So what has changed now, Gautam? Are you both back together?"

After a deep thought, Gautam replied, "I actually don't know where she stands regarding us being together. I have no idea whether she will even forgive and accept me back in her life. But I have decided that I can't stay without her. So I am getting myself transferred back to India and the first thing that I will do when I reach Mumbai is ask her to marry me."

Gautam held Payal's hand but did not have the courage to look her in the eyes. "I really like you, Payal. With you, I can be myself. Please forgive me, if you can. You know, when I left Mumbai, I made a huge mistake by not speaking or discussing my apprehensions with Roshni, and I ended our relationship in the worst way possible because I was scared. I promised myself that I would not repeat such a mistake again because that is the worst thing that you can do in a relationship – one fine day, just stop talking without giving any reason."

Payal could sense the remorse in Gautam's trembling voice and gave him a comforting and reassuring hug.

"Payal, I don't want to lose you as a friend. I have cherished a lot of fond memories with you, and I will be grateful if you will forgive me and accept me as a friend."

Payal knew what Gautam did to her could not be undone, especially with the feelings she had for him. But he was brave enough to tell her everything honestly, rather than running away from the situation. Her respect for Gautam went up a notch due to his sincerity about their friendship.

Payal replied, "I will be your friend for life, Gautam, and I really hope that Roshni accepts you back and agrees to marry you. Just in case she needs a reference, you can always call me," Payal concluded with a smile to reduce the tension in the emotional discussion and wished him all the best for the future.

Roshni patted Gautam's back in appreciation after he finished sharing the details of his conversation with Payal. "In the past month, I think you have matured a lot, and I am absolutely loving the new and improved Gautam."

Roshni and Gautam kissed. They were back together, engaged and madly in love with each other.

ONCE THE REALISATION SUNK IN THAT THEY WERE engaged and together, then began the excited phone calls to friends to share the good news.

Gautam first called his best friend, Rohit, and informed him of the development.

Rohit was taken aback by the news as he assumed Gautam would be in Singapore, but at the same time he was also pleased for him.

"Buddy, I tried my best to dissuade you, but if you still feel so strongly about Roshni, then it is indeed true love," Rohit said with a chuckle. "So, when is the wedding? Let me know soon so I can book my tickets accordingly." Rohit was barely able to hold his excitement. "Because of you, at least, I will get an excuse to come to India."

At the same time, Roshni was talking on the phone with her close friend, Sonal, who too put forward the same question. She and Gautam looked at each other with a 'how did we forget' expression. It suddenly registered to them that they had not discussed the date, as they were yet to inform Gautam's parents and get their approval and blessings.

"What a rookie mistake," Gautam blamed himself loudly. "Just when I thought I was beginning to understand emotions better, I make another blunder." He informed Rohit that he would let him know soon about the date and hung up quickly.

"The easier part of asking you is over but now the more difficult part – convincing my parents about my love for you – is left," Gautam informed Roshni in a worried tone. "I think we should meet them today evening. I don't want to delay telling them. I have not even informed them that I am back in India, and once I reach home, I am sure they will know something is up."

After a few minutes thinking about their strategy, they decided that it would be prudent for Gautam to call his sister and inform her. Richa had to be the one to get their parents to understand Gautam's perspective.

Richa was surprised and jubilant when Gautam's Indian phone number flashed on her screen. "Gautam, what an amazing surprise! I thought you were not going to be back for a year. We were all missing you so much."

"Hey, sister, I missed you guys too. I have some great news to share," replied Gautam in excitement over what he was about to tell his sister. "It's a long story but in short, the reason for me coming here was to propose to Roshni and yes, sis, I am so happy to inform you that she agreed. I am over the moon. This is the best day of my life!"

"Whoa, brother, that was so romantic of you. I can't believe my little brother has become so mature and spontaneous. So I assume you are absolutely sure about the relationship now?" Richa was glad that Gautam had finally decided the way forward.

"Yes I am, no doubts whatsoever. But there is just one little problem… our parents," Gautam ended with a sigh.

"I am planning to take Roshni to meet them this evening. I need you to be there with us. We need your support to convince mom and dad. Please help us out."

Gautam's insisting pleas melted Richa's heart and she agreed to be there without fail. She had promised her brother that she would stand by him whatever his decision. It was time to walk the talk.

Gautam kept the phone down and saw Roshni walking anxiously in the living room. "Should I be nervous, Gautam? How would your parents react after meeting me? They would have never thought in their wildest dreams that their son would want to marry an older woman like me." Roshni looked like she was losing her cool worrying about what could unfold in the evening.

She curbed herself from asking Gautam the dreaded question of what would happen if they did not agree to their marriage. Would he leave her for good or would he leave his parents to be with her? Both situations would tear Roshni apart. She wanted to remain as positive as possible and prayed that everything would turn out fine.

Gautam's father, Baldev Batra was a typical Punjabi in his attitudes – large hearted with a 'don't care a damn' attitude about social norms. He had migrated to Mumbai from the city of Ludhiana just after finishing his studies, hoping to make it big in the city of dreams. He lived life on his own terms and in most cases went against the norms of society. After coming to Mumbai and a lot of rejections later, he got a job in a stockbroking firm, a field which even today, continues to be dominated by the highly enterprising Gujarati community. But despite the language barrier, he still managed to reach the top of the organisation with sheer willpower and determination to succeed. He even learnt how to converse in Gujarati fluently.

Then, one day after five years of working there, he decided it was time for him to start his own broking firm. He did that with aplomb, established himself and, in the interim, also ended up marrying his lady luck – his ex-boss's daughter.

Gautam's mother, Snehal Batra had stood by her husband through all the ups and downs of business and life. She too had a good knowledge of the stock market and was a great partner for him. Though she was an integral part of her children's lives growing up, Mrs Batra spent quite some time in the office to help her husband in the business as well.

Gautam hardly spent any time with his father during his school days, but they developed a greater fondness for each other when he was in college, bonding over sports, especially cricket and football. They might not have had the most friendliest of relations, but Gautam had immense respect for his father for the way he had tirelessly worked for the family and given both, him and his sister, the independence to follow their dreams and aspirations. Gautam was closer emotionally to his mother and shared all his fears and desires with her. But for him, the closest in the family was Richa, his elder sister, who was practically like a second mother to him.

Gautam was unsure about how his parents would react. It was very difficult to predict as the situation they were in was not a common one. Even though he would take advice from his father on academic and career decisions, he was not as emotionally open with him as he was with his mother. He was counting on the fact that his father too, had not followed the set societal norms his entire life.

As the famous saying goes, "Like father, like son."

Gautam and Roshni spent the rest of the afternoon a little worried and tense, not knowing what was in store for them in the evening. Gautam left for home after lunch, around 5 p.m. so that he could get his parents in a good mood before breaking the big news to them in the evening. It was decided that Roshni would reach Gautam's residence by 8 p.m.

It took an hour for Gautam to reach his home as he stopped at the Siddhivinayak temple to get the Almighty's blessings for things to go down well in the evening's crucial meeting.

His parents were pleasantly surprised to see him back without any intimation. He had never been away so long from them. There were long hugs with his parents, and his mother had tears of joy in her eyes. He thought to himself that this was a good omen. Considering the good mood his parents were in, they might heed to his request and agree to the marriage.

After spending some time with them, talking about his experiences in Singapore, Gautam excused himself realising it was already past 7 p.m. and Roshni would arrive soon.

"I will just freshen up, mom. I'm feeling a bit tired."

Gautam had steered clear of telling them that he had come back for good and not just a couple of days. He decided it would be better to inform them of all that when the topic of marriage came up later in the evening.

"Yes, you do seem tired, son," his father agreed. "Why don't you hit the bed? We will wake you up in the morning. As per Singapore time, you must be already in sleep mode."

"After a good night's sleep, you will be absolutely fresh," agreed Gautam's mother.

Gautam was surprised by his parent's request. "No, my so lovable and caring parents. I want to spend as much time as possible with the both of you. I missed you so much in Singapore." He was trying his best to get them even more emotional.

"You have changed so much for the better. You must have really yearned for us a lot," said Mrs Batra tearing up again.

"But tell me, son, what brings you here all of a sudden?" asked his father in a serious tone.

This was not the question that Gautam wanted to reply to yet, so he tried his best to be as evasive as possible.

"Some work, Dad. I will tell you over dinner," he replied and started to walk away from the living room to avoid further probing.

"Okay, son. I have some news for you too, that I will give you at the dinner table," said his father. It was like a thunderbolt leaving Gautam perplexed as he entered his room.

He thought to himself, "What news would they have to give me? Since I am out of the house now, are they thinking of getting a pet dog I was dead against or are they looking at selling this apartment and moving somewhere else? What else? What else?" It suddenly hit him. "Are they trying to hook me up with someone else for marriage?" Gautam got into panic mode but managed to gather himself. Nothing could shake his determination.

"No, dad, before you throw the bouncer at me, I will throw you mine," he thought to himself.

Gautam unpacked his stuff and took a nice, hot shower. He got into a fresh pair of denims and a smart dark blue t-shirt. As Gautam entered the living room, he found his parents already seated there with big smiles on their faces.

Gautam knew something was up. With his parents smiling like that, it must surely be about a marriage proposal, he thought to himself. Before his father could tell him the news, he decided to announce his own first. "So, dad, you wanted to know the real purpose why I came, right?"

"Oh, forget it. I have an announcement to make before that." His father appeared least bothered by Gautam's reasons for coming, leaving him even more anxious.

"No way, dad, first I have to tell you–" Gautam was cut off by his father before he could finish his sentence.

"I am not interested." His father raised his hand as if to calm Gautam down, who was getting irritated. "Mr Mehra, my close friend, has offered his daughter's hand for you."

This time, it was Gautam's turn to cut his father off. "Dad, I am in love with Roshni, and I want to marry her. There, I said it. That's why I have come here. I love Roshni, and I want to marry her."

"Let me at least complete my sentence, son. Mr Mehra offered, but I said no because you are in love with Roshni and want to marry her."

Gautam was stunned as his parents burst out laughing looking at him.

"Roshni, our daughter, can you please come in?" requested Gautam's mother. Gautam was left dumbfounded. He simply could not believe what he was hearing. He and Roshni had agonised all afternoon about the outcome of their meeting with his parents, and here, without saying a word, everything was already taken care of.

Roshni entered the living room with Richa, looking like the ideal daughter-in-law, dressed in a beautiful blue sari.

Gautam was overcome with emotions as he hugged his parents and touched their feet, tears of joy rolling down his eyes. "Mom, dad, you are the best. Thanks a lot. This is the best gift you could have ever given us—your acceptance of our relationship."

He then went over to Roshni with excitement written all over him. "I told you, not to be so nervous. My parents are damn cool."

"Yes, right," Roshni said in a sarcastic tone and pinched him.

After some calmness was restored and pleasantries were exchanged, Gautam politely asked his parents, "But Mom and Dad, how did you agree so fast? You do know that she is twelve years older than me, right?"

Roshni was embarrassed. Richa, on the other hand, looked cross.

"What are you trying to do, Gautam? Confuse them and make them change their decision, which I so successfully derived after convincing them for over two hours? After speaking to you, I came over immediately to speak to them over lunch," she said in an irritated voice. "I had a very interesting and long discussion, clearing all their doubts. It seemed as if I was the one wanting to get married and not you."

Richa went on to explain what had transpired between her and their parents.

Soon after Gautam's call, Richa decided to rush over to her parents' house. Normally their parents would not have any objections in accepting any partner that Gautam wanted to marry. But she was sure that they would definitely find it difficult to accept a woman twelve years elder to Gautam as his life partner and their daughter-in-law. Reaching before her brother would give her the opportunity to discuss the decision with their parents in a practical way without emotions running high. It would also give them time for the decision to sink in, rather than their son hitting them with such big news out of the blue. It is human tendency to be evasive to sudden announcements especially when they are considered to be negative.

Richa informed her mother over phone that she would be coming over for lunch. It took her nearly an hour to reach. Half an hour later with lunch done, the three of them made themselves comfortable on the ivory coloured sofa set in the living room with Richa and her mother sitting next to each other while her father occupied the seat opposite them.

"I have some big news for you, mom and dad," Richa started off. "Your son has found his match, the woman of his dreams. He has been in a serious relationship for the past four months and today they decided that they want to take the next step and get married."

"For a while I thought you were pregnant again and that's why you came over for lunch," remarked Richa's father with a smile.

"This is excellent news and I am so happy for him. What's her name ? What does she do ? But just out of curiosity why are you breaking the news to us and not him?" Mr Batra was all excited with the pleasant information which he wasn't expecting on a lazy Sunday afternoon especially with their son in Singapore.

"I agree, this is great news for the family. However I am surprised that he did not even once mention to me anything about this girl. That hurts a bit." Gautam always had an open relation with his mother keeping no secrets from her. Such a major decision in life was taken by him without taking her into confidence, set Mrs Batra back a little, though she was still happy for him.

"I am also curious though, why have you specially come home to break this news to us?" asked Richa's mother.

Richa took a deep breath before giving her reply as she knew a long conversation, maybe even a heated one, was going to follow.

"The woman, Gautam is in love with is Roshni and they were working together in the same office of Global Bank before he moved to Singapore. She is rather his senior and Gautam even used to report to her for certain projects."

"Wow, and I thought Gautam was young and doing well in his career. Roshni is one step ahead. She must be his age or younger and Gautam reports to her. I must say that I am truly impressed." Mr Batra was working on the assumption that Roshni was his son's age.

"Dad, Roshni is older than Gautam. She is thirty-seven but doesn't look her age," said Richa nonchalantly, trying not to make a big deal out of it.

"What? Are you serious? Is this a joke? He bloody wants to get married to a divorcee. What will everyone say in society? What will our relatives say? Where is that rascal? I want to speak to him right away. No wonder that rat has sent you rather than being here himself!" Mr Batra was all worked up, fuming in anger.

"Dad, will you cool down and stop speaking about Gautam in a derogatory way? Roshni is neither a divorcee nor is she married. She is a single, smart and independent woman. Gautam took quite some time to decide on the long term implications of such an age gap relationship. He had even spoken to me in detail about his doubts. He truly loves Roshni. But foremost he loves his parents and without your permission or consent he will not marry anyone." Richa was trying her best to calm the parents down. Before she could explain to them how Gautam and Roshni's relationship came around, her mother cut in.

"Richa, I know Gautam is an emotional person but we have to be practical and straight on his behalf. He might be blind in love but we are not. We as parents have to correct our children if we find them straying in a wrong direction. I could have still understood an age difference of one or two years but twelve is impractical. Look around in the society, do you find such kind of relationships anywhere except maybe between the film stars or celebrities who can get away with anything. The reason is because it is impractical and an impossible relationship to maintain."

"What are your apprehensions, mom and dad? I know you are outraged with this sudden development but think calmly and tell me." Richa knew that in order to get over this shock, it was important to get her parents to speak about the topic and vent out their frustrations.

"The first thing everyone is going to ask us is, why is a young boy like Gautam marrying a thirty-seven year old woman? Is she rich? Is she helping the growth of his career? Someone might say, not me but someone else, is she too hot for him to resist? Is she a cougar who digs young men? The tongues are going to wag. What are we going to say?" Gautam's father was a straightforward man who never minced his words. He said things as he saw it. No diplomacy there.

"I think there is only one thing to say to people who will ask you this," replied Richa, "that your son is truly in love and age does not matter. If Roshni was the same age as Gautam, then she would have been considered the best girl in the world but just because she is thirty-seven, there has be something wrong with her and there has to be an ulterior motive. That is such shallow thinking. People love to talk and to gossip, dad and they can do so about anything. Tongues can wag for even Gautam going to Singapore for his one year stint – maybe he does not get along with his parents and that's why he grabbed the first opportunity that came along to move away. Can you stop people from saying that? If Gautam's intentions are clear and noble, that the only reason he wishes to marry Roshni is that they love each other, then we have to support him rather than be influenced by what others think."

Mrs Batra finding her husband being cornered by Richa's sweet talk intervened. "Richa, it is not just that. If you are talking about marriage, then what about having children? She being thirty-seven is going to have a tough time in conceiving a child. What about Gautam? When does he want to become a father? They will always have this sword hanging over them. It can't be too late for one and too early for the other. Where is the middle ground? What about maturity levels, emotional connect, similar wavelengths on everything they do or decide. Once the physical attraction fades off, they have to connect mentally."

"Mom, every husband and wife faces these questions. For some the answers are simple and for some complex. The timing of when to have children is a debate which happens with all couples and more often than not, one of them always feels that it is either too early or too late. I had this on-going debate with my husband for nearly two years before we went ahead with Aarav being born. But he still feels till today that we became parents too soon for his liking. Yes, her age will be a stumbling block in conceiving but with the advancement of technology I don't think it is as much a challenge as it used be years ago.

My personal opinion about your other doubts of maturity, emotional connect and general compatibility is that if a problem has to happen it can happen with a partner of any age. I find couples of similar ages disagree more because when they are young or new in marriage, they tend not to reason things but behave as if they are just two separate people, now living under the same roof. Making adjustments for each other is not high on priority. Gautam on the other hand is lucky I feel in that regard, since Roshni being elder, will bring a sense of maturity and calmness in his life." Richa was trying her best to give the most apt answers to her parents' queries hoping to make them see the relationship in a positive light. Somewhere Richa's answers were having the desired effect which was irritating them all the more.

Not ready to accept the situation yet, Gautam's father again spoke out, "Richa everything is not as simple as you are trying to make it out to be. What about old age companionship? You have to be mentally ready that she will not be alive when Gautam is going to be old. Will Gautam also be able to handle the income and stature difference that he has with Roshni? Men generally don't take kindly to that sort of disparity where woman is on top."

"Dad, as far as your first question is concerned, as per a United Nations survey women tend to live on an average five years more than men. In case of India, even more. We have an example of that in our own house. Our naani lived ten years longer than our naanu. Did she get bored or stop enjoying her life? We were all there with her till the end. Isn't that what families do? Support each other. I don't think Gautam will have issues regarding that. Even if he has, don't worry I will always be there with him.

As for your other question, you just sounded like a typical old generation male chauvinist. Things have changed in the last decade. Today men and women are equal and I don't think men in general harbour such bias towards the women they love. India has had a woman President, Prime Minister and even a Defence Minister. Women are bringing so many accolades for the country in sports. If the men across India can accept women leading us in various walks of life, I am sure Gautam has no such qualms." Richa had come prepared for the discussion and the queries put up by her parents were in line with what she had assumed. The answers from her side were prompt and to the point.

Richa took hold of her mother's hand and gave it a reassuring squeeze. "I totally understand your reaction, mom and dad. I too was taken aback by Gautam's decision when he told me the first time. Your apprehensions are more to do with the answers, the explanations that you will have to give your relatives and the society in general. You both went against the society norms, with a Punjabi marrying a Gujarati in those days against the wishes of mom's family. You never cared for what others thought because you loved and trusted each other and that is what ultimately matters.

If you believe in your son and in the choice he makes, you will overlook the age factor. After all isn't age just a number. I know my brother inside out and I am sure he will not marry anyone unless you both agree. Hence it is very important for you to happily say yes to this marriage. It will mean the world to him."

Mr Batra with a wry smile shook his head at the irony of the situation, "He could have decided to marry anyone and we would have had no anxiety or concern. I guess what goes round does come around. Things would have been so much simpler had he been in a normal relationship. Richa, you have made things sound so straightforward and clear. For once, I hate that. We indeed are going to have a tough time explaining things to people but as you pointed out, we care more about our son's feelings rather than the feelings of the society. If we ignore the age difference, then Roshni seems to be the most apt woman that Gautam could have chosen as his wife."

Mrs Batra agreed with her husband's assessment, "I am sure if Gautam would have announced his intention in person, it would have been a shouting match between father and the son. I am so happy you did the difficult work on behalf of your younger brother, Richa. You have always been there for him. I love my children so much and I am very proud of the bond they share with each other." Her eyes welled up in pride for her daughter and son. She composed herself and asked Richa, "Tell me something more about Roshni. How did they fall in love?"

Richa briefed her parents about Roshni and Gautam's first meeting, they falling in love, Gautam's introspection of the relationship when challenged by Rohit, their breakup and finally Gautam's proposal. She also gave them a detailed explanation of Roshni's tragic past and her career growth.

"I so want to meet Roshni. Can you ask her to come over, Richa?" queried an overwhelmed Mrs Batra who was now very excited to meet their future daughter-in-law.

"To tell you the truth, I have yet to meet her as well. But you have a surprise in store. Gautam is on the way home and Roshni should be here for dinner later. I too was supposed to join them for dinner but I thought it would be wiser for me to come earlier and meet you both before they did. So please act surprised when he comes. In the meantime I will ask Roshni to meet me in a nearby cafe and then bring her home while Gautam goes to his room to freshen up."

Richa had a plan ready to catch his brother off guard and surprise him. It also gave her parents an opportunity to interact with Roshni in person alone and clear any remaining apprehensions.

"Son, we love you, and the person you wish to marry has to be loved and adored by us too. Initially, we were shocked and had our doubts. We met Roshni while you were freshening up and I absolutely understand why you fell head over heels for her. She is a wonderful human being." Gautam's mother explained.

His father continued, "Richa discussed everything with us and explained the emotional turbulence that you went through before finally deciding to propose to Roshni. After hearing all of that, we thought 'what the hell.' In your happiness lies our happiness and you are old enough to take your own decisions. Moreover at this stage of our lives we did not want to be the reason for your heart break. We don't know how many years we have ahead of us but they have to be spent together with joy and contentment in the company of our children and grandchildren."

Gautam went to his parents and embraced them. He truly appreciated the fact that it was not easy for them to accept his relationship with Roshni owing to their age gulf. Gautam then hugged his sister tightly. "You are really good. In fact, too good." His joy knew no bounds, and neither did Roshni's.

As they proceeded towards the dining table, Gautam, who was especially eager to get married soon, casually asked his mother, "So when is the right time to get married?"

"Exactly six weeks from today is ideal," was the instant reply. "Unless you two are in no hurry."

Gautam had earlier thought that they would marry within a year of the engagement. But the last few weeks of separation from Roshni had made him change his decision. Now he was in a hurry to get married and start a new chapter in his life with her as soon as possible. He did not want any more negative influences coming between their love.

"My parents are the best," said a beaming Gautam. "What say, Roshni? That gives us around a month to prepare. Is your schedule clear?"

"Who am I to go against your parents' wishes," replied Roshni as the entire family celebrated over dinner, Gautam's homecoming as well as his impending wedding to Roshni.

ONCE THE DATE FOR THEIR WEDDING WAS FIXED, IT seemed that Gautam and Roshni could not keep their feet on the ground. Both were madly in love and could not bear to stay away from each other. Their phone calls got longer, and meetings regular, despite their busy schedules. Clubbing on the weekends until the wee hours of the morning, along with lavish and romantic dinners, had become a norm. However, after a month, this hectic schedule started taking a toll on Roshni's health. She had never experienced such a lifestyle earlier and that coupled with the shortened hours of sleep had a tiring effect on her body, even affecting her work efficiency.

Gautam called Roshni to fix up the time to meet on Friday night, just a week prior to their wedding.

"I am not feeling that well. Just a little down today. Maybe tomorrow?" pleaded Roshni. She wanted to avoid exerting herself a week before the wedding.

"Please, Roshni, it's Friday night, and all my old school friends are meeting up after ages. I have said so many great things about you that they are all very excited to meet up. Please, please, please make it," requested Gautam frantically.

"I can't, my love. Would have loved to meet them, but today my entire body is enveloped in pain. I even left the office early, as I was not feeling well and might be running a fever. Extremely sorry, dear."

Roshni was at home, trying to relax on her bed after popping a pill for the fever.

"Okay, Rosh, no worries. If you want me to come over to check on you, I will be there later in the evening. Otherwise, I will see you tomorrow. Love you." With this, he hung up on a sad note, after being told by Roshni to go ahead and not worry about her. She was a big girl and could take care of herself.

The next day, Roshni could not even get up from bed. She was running a high fever, and was shivering in pain. It was eight in the morning, and she knew that Gautam would still be sleeping after the late night. She instead called her best friend, Sonal, asking her to bring some medicines over.

Sonal was her closest, and probably the only friend from her college days. She and her family had been a great support to Roshni after her parents passed away. Roshni had even stayed with her for a few weeks after the tragic accident. Sonal, a music teacher by profession was married to her college sweetheart, who was quite a popular vocalist. She lived only four lanes away from Roshni and hence was very easily accessible.

"You are lucky that I had a day off today," said Sonal as she entered the apartment with the extra set of keys she had. "So how come all of a sudden you have such high fever? Or, should I say, love fever?"

"You can actually say that," replied Roshni in a tired voice. "The number of outings we have been having – the late nights, the dancing, the partying – I am feeling totally worn out. I just want to rest for a few days or else I will look tired for my own wedding."

Sonal helped Roshni sit up in her bed to eat the breakfast that she had brought with her. It was just a few slices of bread and butter to put some energy back into Roshni.

"I wanted to ask you this before, Roshni, but I don't know whether this is the right time or the right question," asked Sonal in a worried tone. "Have you really thought this decision through to marry Gautam, who is twelve years younger than you? I know, you are growing old and when a man as good as Gautam proposes, it is immensely difficult to say no, but do you think there are enough common grounds? You both are supposed to grow old together but here you are in bed, broken down from too much fun and Gautam, I guess he needs more. Are you going to be able to keep up with his youthful exuberance?" Sonal could no longer hold back her concerns, looking at the state in which Roshni was, and seeing that Gautam was nowhere to be found. She had been Roshni's close confidante for more than two decades and was protective of her.

She continued with her issues. "And then at night after marriage, he is going to be like a machine," she chuckled. "Will you be able to satisfy him regularly? Or just have sex once a week, like we do at this age with partners of our age? When we were young, even half a day was too long for my husband to stay away from me. If you don't heed to them, they get unnecessarily cranky. Moreover, the worst case scenario is that, if you don't satisfy him, then he will have to find other women to quench his urges. Thus, you are creating mistrust, which is the beginning of a breakup. When you reach the age of sixty, he will be forty-eight and still active. What do you do then?"

It was the Rohit talk all over again, it seemed, though the sermon-giver this time was Sonal, and the receiver, Roshni. The only change was the difference in perspectives from a man's to a woman's. Sonal had met Gautam only a couple of times as they had been on double dates, but was yet to warm up to him. Maybe it was just because of their age difference that their perspectives did not match.

Sonal continued with her views, "Do your interests even match? I mean, you like being home, and he likes going out; you want to read books, he wants to watch movies; you like art and he… well, the less said, the better.

All your friends, including me, have kids. Imagine Gautam coming along with all of us. Do you think he can fit in? He is not used to being called an uncle at all. Being called that might put him into a coma, for all you know." Sonal let out a chuckle and continued.

"You have one outlook of life, and he has the exact opposite. You want to plan your children's upbringing in a particular way, while he might have something else in mind – that is, if he wants children in the first place. What about the difference in your status and income? Is Gautam reconciled to the fact that at work he will always be a level below you? People are invariably going to find you as an odd couple and question the basis of your relationship. Both of you will have to be thick skinned and learn to laugh it off when you come across such uncomfortable situations. You are lucky that Gautam's parents did not baulk at your age gap and throw tantrums about accepting you as their daughter-in-law. But the real test will be when you start living with them. For a younger woman to mould her ways in accordance with the family she moves into, is easier. But for you it is not going to be simple especially since you have been living independently without being answerable to anyone."

Roshni, instead of feeling better after eating breakfast and taking the medicines, was feeling the opposite owing to the new thoughts her best friend had introduced. But before she could start replying to Sonal, the doorbell rang and it was her love, Gautam – a face she was so eager to see. Roshni was smiling again, forgetting everything that Sonal had mentioned a few minutes earlier.

"Hi, Sonal. Thanks for keeping her company," Gautam acknowledged Sonal and gave her a hug.

"Why did you not call me, Roshni? I would have stayed home with you last night and taken care of you, instead of partying. In a week's time, I have a vow to take of being there with you in sickness and in health for the rest of your life. We could have started practicing from yesterday itself," said Gautam with a twinkle in his eyes.

This brought a big smile to Roshni's face, which had gone sullen after listening to Sonal's predictions.

"I will leave you two alone. Bye, both of you." Sonal went to hug Roshni, who was still on the bed, and whispered into her ears, "Do think about what I said Roshni, seriously and clear the doubts with Gautam."

She then quickly left the apartment.

"What was she talking about?" asked a curious Gautam.

"She just wanted my advice on some financial matters," replied Roshni in a low guilty voice, as she was hiding the truth from him.

"So, what happened to you all of a sudden?" asked a worried Gautam.

"Maybe the late nights and partying got to my ageing body," replied Roshni, with a little pain in her tone.

"Let's take it easy, then. We will just stay put at home today, maybe watch some TV together, and we'll round it off with a quiet dinner here. You rest well, and since tomorrow is Sunday, we can spend it your way. The way you want it," said Gautam at his supportive best.

"Well, that already makes me feel good," Roshni responded cheerfully, already feeling better with Gautam's comforting words.

"So what will we be doing on your Sunday?" asked an inquisitive Gautam.

"Let's keep that as a surprise," replied Roshni with a wry smile. She wanted to get better before planning anything.

"Now I am suddenly not feeling well," said Gautam, as they broke into a round of laughter.

Saturday went by as the love birds had planned. Roshni got all the rest she needed and was back on her feet, although still a little weak. Gautam had taken extremely good care of her, ensuring that she was properly rested and medicated. The entire day was spent at home watching TV, catching up on some movies, playing a few board games and generally chatting with each other. Roshni felt vastly comforted with Gautam's caring behaviour, which reinforced her love for him.

True to his promise of spending Sunday the way Roshni wanted to, Gautam was back at her place early in the morning. He had left the previous night at 10:30 p.m. after ensuring Roshni was in bed and about to sleep. He returned early in the morning with breakfast from her favourite South Indian restaurant.

"You are really determined to please me, Gautam," said Roshni on opening the door. She was up early, feeling well rested, and had already taken a bath.

"Since you were sick, I have to help you cheer up, which is my moral duty. Otherwise, who in their right senses would wake up at 6.30 a.m. on a holiday."

Even though it was an early Sunday morning for him, Gautam was in good spirits and felt proud of how well he had taken care of Roshni.

"So where are we off to first, dear?" queried a smiling Gautam. He was glad to be moving outdoors after spending the previous day at home.

"First, we go to the Jehangir Art Gallery. They have showcased the early paintings of M.F. Hussain, and I am dying to see them." Roshni had planned the entire day before Gautam arrived.

"What? We are going to the art museum?" frowned Gautam.

Noticing Roshni's angry looks, he quickly changed his stance, "Of course, anything for you, darling. Just anything," said Gautam in a nervous tone.

They quickly finished the South Indian delicacies of dosa and idli and headed off to the gallery in South Mumbai which was an hour's drive away.

Roshni, who had a keen eye for paintings, was deeply engrossed in studying them one after the other. Gautam, on the other hand, was not an art admirer and had no clue about them. He just kept shaking his head in acknowledgement of whatever Roshni explained about the artwork. He deliberately stayed a step behind her, so that she could not see his bored and sleepy face.

After some time, as Roshni neared the last set of paintings, she realised that Gautam was no longer with her. She was worried and started looking out for him.

After searching him for couple of minutes, she finally found Gautam sleeping in a particularly embarrassing position on a chair in the reception, with one leg spread out on the armrest, his mouth wide open and his loud snoring acting as a musical background. Roshni was annoyed to see Gautam in that state, especially when he was supposed to be giving her company. She shook him and, after a few moments, Gautam reluctantly opened his eyes.

"What are you doing there, my beloved wife? Come and sleep besides me," responded Gautam, still in sleep mode and eyes barely open.

"Gautam, you are not in your bed but in the art gallery," said Roshni in a highly embarrassed low tone.

The situation slowly dawned upon Gautam and he sheepishly got up from the chair. Head down, he followed Roshni out of the building without a word.

Once they were outside, Gautam acknowledged his mistake and offered his sincere apologies to Roshni.

"I am so sorry, Rosh. I just went to relax my legs, which had become tired of walking and standing, and before I knew it, I had dozed off. Please forgive me. This will definitely not happen again."

Seeing the genuineness of the apology and his sorry face, Roshni's smile was back. "But please don't do that again," she told him lovingly but firmly.

"Yes, madam," replied Gautam with determination. "So where to next?"

"Now for a woman's dream way of spending her Sunday," replied Roshni with glee while clapping her hands.

"Go on, I am all ears," said an excited Gautam. He was hoping that Roshni would have planned a spa date to help relax their bodies. It would be the ideal way to spend a Sunday, he thought.

Roshni, however, had other ideas. "Arm in arm with her love for a round of shopping."

"What!" exclaimed Gautam, his smile disappearing again.

"Yes, I need to buy my dress for the engagement party, and who better to choose the dress than the one who will be by my side throughout?"

From South Mumbai, they drove down to Lower Parel arriving into Phoenix Mills, probably the biggest shopping mall in Mumbai.

Then started the tedious and comical process of going from one shop to the other, rejecting various dresses for varied reasons, buying many, and in Gautam's opinion unnecessary women's accessories. The end result, after three nightmarish hours, was that Gautam had five huge bags to carry.

Roshni noticed that Gautam was hardly interested in her dresses or shopping and was no longer paying attention to what she was saying. He was busy on his phone most of the time and looked happier when on it, rather than when giving his opinion to her. She was beginning to rethink what Sonal had told her about the differences which could start creeping up as their relationship progressed, owing to their age gap.

"Oh, come on, Roshni, for god's sake, just buy a dress and let's move on. I am hungry, my feet are hurting, and I am about to go to sleep again. I think this dress is perfect and you look ravishing in it. Please buy it, I beg you." Gautam had gone from a happy mood to an irritated one. Those five-six hours that Sunday had been the longest and most excruciating ones of his life. He had never felt so bored.

Roshni heeded his advice grudgingly, although she did not openly display it as she wanted to avoid an argument.

They finally moved on and into the Italian-cuisine restaurant California Pizza Kitchen which was within the shopping complex itself.

At the restaurant, Gautam was excessively distracted as he could not take his eyes off the English Premier League football match, which was being shown live on the TV. Roshni now was in a sombre mood as Sonal's words kept hitting her again and again.

"Gautam, we need to speak," Roshni began their conversation, wanting to explain to him that his behaviour was not what she expected.

"Yes, tell me," replied Gautam casually, his eyes stuck on the match.

Before Roshni could utter another word, the football match got interesting as Gautam's favourite team Arsenal's goal was disallowed by the referee. He could not stop cursing thereafter.

"I think the table near the TV is free. We should shift there," he got up and walked off without bothering to seek Roshni's confirmation.

Roshni dragged herself to the other table. They had their late lunch while watching the match and hardly a word was spoken between them.

Gautam was still animated about how his team had lost the match when they left the restaurant. After not getting any response from Roshni, it finally registered to him that she was not in a good mood and had been way too quiet for some time.

"So, Roshni, you wanted to talk about something at the restaurant? Listen, before that, let me again apologise to you for my earlier behaviour. I was dead tired and bored of shopping. I just vented my frustration without thinking. Sorry again."

It was Gautam's third apology of the day, and he seemed to have mastered the act.

Gautam's expression of regret melted her heart, and Roshni just shook her head, smiled at him and replied, "I just wanted to say that I forgive you. We still have time, so let's watch a movie."

"Yes, boss, whatever you say," said Gautam, reverting back to his enthusiastic ways. A nice, fun movie was what he needed after a long, dull and monotonous day to cheer him up and end it on a high.

PHOENIX MILLS WAS A RETAIL SHOPPING HUB, WHERE everyone from South Mumbai would throng. Apart from the wide number of branded showrooms and restaurants it housed, there was also a seven-screen PVR cinema – the biggest movie theatre chain in the country – inside it. This was where Roshni and Gautam were headed.

Since it was a Sunday, they were greeted with a long queue for tickets outside the theatre. Gautam volunteered to drop all the shopping bags to the car, which was in the parking lot of the mall. Roshni, in the meantime, was to get the movie tickets.

After fifteen minutes of standing in the queue, Roshni finally managed to get the two tickets. She came back and again stood near the beginning of the line, around where both of them had parted ways. This way, she thought, Gautam could easily find her. After a couple of minutes, she saw Gautam coming back with a big smile.

"Hey, we got the tickets," said Gautam excitedly.

They entered the theatre, both presenting two tickets each to two different guards as the men and women security check lines were separate. Neither had taken note that they now had four tickets, instead of two.

"I was so looking forward to watching this movie," said Gautam gleefully.

"So was I," agreed Roshni.

They got off the escalator, which had taken them to one level above the main entrance. Both looked at their tickets and started moving in opposite directions, assuming the other would automatically follow. After a few seconds of walking ahead, both realised that they were walking alone.

"Our screen is this side," shouted Gautam. He waved at Roshni to get her attention.

"No, it's here," she yelled back.

Gautam went over to where she was standing.

Both of them simultaneously spoke up, while waving their tickets at each other.

"Star Trek Beyond is on Screen Seven," said Gautam.

"Rustom is on Screen Five," said Roshni.

"I was supposed to buy the tickets," frowned Roshni.

"When I came back, I saw you standing where I left you. I thought that maybe you did not get the tickets due to the long queue and hence you were still there. Coincidentally, I met this couple who had extra tickets, and I bought them. It is a movie which I wanted to see so badly. All my friends have been raving about it. So let's go, please," Gautam pleaded to get Roshni to see his preferred movie.

"No, I want to watch the Hindi movie, Rustom, with my favourite actor, Akshay Kumar; not some sci-fi crap," Roshni shot back at Gautam, irritated with his behaviour.

"What is the movie about?" inquired Gautam to see if the story could hold some interest for him.

"It is about a decorated naval officer who comes to know that his wife is cheating on him and goes on to kill his wife's lover, leading to a sensational trial over passion versus premeditated murder. It is based on a real incident that happened in Mumbai in the late 1950s, which led to the end of jury trials in India," Roshni responded, giving all details of the movie, hoping it would appeal to Gautam.

"It sounds too monotonous. Anyways, who wants to see the past when you can see the future in Star Trek?" Gautam said in defence of his movie.

They both stood there, staring at each other, neither ready to give in.

"I am boldly going where no man has ever gone before, leaving his girl to watch a movie alone," said Gautam and turned towards his screen.

Halfway to the screen, realising that he was alone again and Roshni had called his bluff, he turned back and ran to her, "It's your day today, so we do what you say."

Gautam understood in time that he was a thorough gentleman and could not just leave his woman stranded. Roshni, on the other hand, was about to blow her fuse, which she had been controlling the entire day. Gautam's turnaround in the nick of time saved what could have been potentially their first big argument.

They entered the movie hall, hands held tightly.

Halfway through the movie, Roshni laid her head on Gautam's shoulder in a nice romantic gesture, only to notice that he was already asleep. This brought out the anger in her even more, and Sonal's words were back in her mind.

Roshni was lost in her thoughts, trying to make sense of

the entire day. Every activity that day was a challenge, with Gautam apologising for his behaviour every time. One mistake or error of judgment could be overlooked, but not so many. It seemed to her that whenever they did anything Gautam liked, everything was fine between them but the moment her interests were to be prioritised, it was a challenge for Gautam. She was no longer interested in the movie and, with her eyes wide open, she started imagining herself and Gautam as characters in the film.

Roshni, portraying herself as a fifty-seven-year-old greying lady, gingerly walked into her bedroom. There, she was shocked to find the forty-five-year-old Gautam making out with a younger woman.

"I have some bad news," remarked Gautam coolly without any remorse, on seeing Roshni. "I will be divorcing you, and I am not even sorry. I am just tired of the word sorry. My life has become a sorry one."

"Why, Gautam, why? What wrong have I done to you? I have always been a good wife," screamed Roshni in an over-the-top reaction.

"I have needs and, since you could not satisfy them due to your old age, I had to, unfortunately, look for greener pastures. We just had too many difference of opinions. The age gap screwed us," remarked Gautam, while hugging the young girl standing next to him.

"Noooooooo!" screamed Roshni. This startled Gautam into waking up from his deep slumber. They ended up watching the rest of the movie in utter silence. Gautam was under the impression that Roshni's outburst was out of the frustration at seeing him sleep again, instead of enjoying the movie with

her. He was rather scared of her at that moment and decided to keep mum.

Roshni, on the other hand, was embarrassed as the entire audience in the hall had looked in amazement at her. She did not want to make another sound, not even a whisper. The dream had also scared her to no end. Could that ever happen?

"Sorry. I am exceptionally sorry that I went to sleep," said Gautam apologetically as they left the theatre at the end of the movie. Roshni kept silent, even though she was clearly irritated. Saying something back at that time would only worsen the situation. She had to act like the adult in the relationship – she *was* the adult in the relationship. It was the fourth expression of regret from Gautam during the day, Roshni thought to herself in frustration.

Gautam could sense that something was wrong as he had, in fact, irritated her a lot during the day. "She could also be more understanding, though, about my situation," he thought to himself. " Today, she made me do everything I extremely hate. Even yesterday, we were at home the entire day. I hardly slept over the weekend and was back in the morning again on a Sunday. She can't just shout at me like that. She should apologise as well."

Both of them remained silent on the way back. Gautam was to drop Roshni back to her place and then return to his in a taxi. However, Roshni, who was feeling well enough to drive, volunteered to drop Gautam off first as his house was just a ten-minute drive from Phoenix Mills, and then head home. Moreover, she just wanted to be alone with her thoughts after what she believed had been a disastrous day. She was angry with Gautam, and it was better to have some space, she thought to herself.

While he was being dropped, Gautam received a message on his phone from Mr Shim informing him to be in Singapore on Tuesday.

"Roshni, something urgent has come up in the office. I have to leave for Singapore tomorrow night for a couple of days. On Thursday night, Rohit is throwing a bachelor party for me. So all of this means, I will see you directly at the engagement ceremony on Friday. Please do me a favour. Look perfect on that day, just as you are today," said Gautam as he kissed her goodbye.

Misunderstanding and ego were creating a ridge between Roshni and Gautam.

On the way back, Roshni was feeling bad about how the entire day had unfolded in front of her. It was supposed to be the perfect romantic Sunday – the last one before their wedding. Was she expecting too much out of Gautam, who was still only twenty-five years old? He would obviously have some amount of immaturity, given his age, and if she could not see beyond it, then how would their relationship last?

Another question that was thrown at her while watching the movie was whether she would, at any time, feel insecure with Gautam being around women his age. Was there jealousy cropping up in her? What happened between him and Payal could occur again at any time. Would Gautam let it happen once more? Would he be honest and dedicated to her in the future?

Roshni reached home, but all these questions kept her from sleeping. Gautam's two day trip to Singapore provided her the space and time to have a deep thought about their future.

It was her turn to be tormented and to question their relationship.

IT WAS THE NIGHT OF THE ENGAGEMENT. EVEN THOUGH Gautam had already given a ring to Roshni, he had to do it again as a part of the traditional Hindu wedding ceremony in front of his family and friends. Gautam's parents and sister had made all the arrangements to make the event a grand affair. The function was being held at the Blue Sea Banquets in Worli, a place in the vicinity of Gautam's house. The location overlooking the Arabian Sea, was beautifully lit up with scores of colour-changing fairy lights on the coconut trees in the area outside the banquet hall, where an exceedingly elaborate dinner was to be served. There was a cool breeze blowing from the sea, which added to the festive atmosphere.

The hall inside was brightly illuminated and neatly decorated with red and gold drapes running across the twenty-five-feet high ceiling. At one end of the hall, a red carpeted twenty-feet wide stage had been erected, where the formal exchange of rings would take place, after which it would be turned into a dance floor. The stage was, again, attractively done up, with a variety of flower arrangements.

Indian weddings have always been an elaborate family affair and a social PR event, with lots of singing and dancing intermingled with the detailed rituals. No wonder divorce rates in India are among the lowest in the world. After all, who would want to go through the stress of wedding ceremonies again and again?

Gautam and Roshni had reached the hall early and were getting ready in separate changing rooms. Even Gautam had to get a facial done and have his hair set, so he could look perfect that night, given the sheer volume of photos to be taken of the couple.

The week until then had been an extremely hectic and eventful one for Gautam. On Monday night, he left for Singapore for the urgent meeting, which Mr Shim had called to finalise the proposals Gautam and Payal had presented the previous month. The roll out was to begin soon, and the final numbers had to be crunched so that Mr Shim could get the necessary approvals from the bank's headquarters in New York. Gautam along with Payal and the other team members, put in an all-nighter to get the reports ready. Thankfully, everything was completed in time for Gautam to fly back to Mumbai on Thursday morning. On Wednesday night, he had a surprise party thrown for him in the office to celebrate his impending wedding.

The Singapore office was similar to their premises in BKC, Mumbai, and the celebration was held in one of the conference rooms. A small cake was cut to mark the occasion. Payal had taken Gautam's decision in her stride and was in the forefront of arranging the party for him. She had promised Gautam that their friendship would remain intact and seemed to be genuinely happy for him.

Gautam requested Payal to come for his wedding by handing her the invitation card he had specially brought along for her. "I know it is a lot to ask but Payal, please do try coming down to Mumbai for the reception at least. It will mean a lot to me and will be a lot of fun as well. Everyone from the office is going to be there."

Payal hugged Gautam and wished him all the best for his married life. Her parting lines when Gautam was leaving the office for Changi airport were, "I would love to come and be a part of the celebrations. It's just that the work is all piled up here especially with you going on leave. Also I am not sure about facing Ms Roshni yet, as it might be a little awkward given our past. But hey, just in case you decide to change your mind about marrying her, I will be waiting here." There was a naughty smile on her face, and Gautam laughed it off in good humour. Payal it seemed was yet to completely get over her feelings for Gautam.

The next night was the bachelor's party, organised by Rohit. Most of Gautam's close friends from school and college, and a few office colleagues, had been invited. It was a list personally approved by Gautam. Half of a vastly popular lounge in Bandra was booked for the fun and frolic. Beer, vodka and other drinks were flowing endlessly in the crowd, which was mainly a boys-only affair.

The highlight of the night, though, was when an announcement was made in the lounge by Rohit that all the women who danced with Gautam would be served free alcohol. There was nearly a stampede around Gautam and, when the news spread that it was his bachelor's party, he was touched inappropriately by every girl around him. His shyness and embarrassment around them was not helping at all, as it encouraged all the girls to be naughtier.

Roshni, on the other hand, had a relatively quiet time. She had to complete the last-minute alterations of her engagement and wedding dresses, along with packing her entire trousseau as she would be moving into Gautam's residence after marriage. The decision had been debated by the couple a lot, but Roshni insisted that it would be wiser for them to stay with his parents for at least a year and then decide if they wanted to live independently. She did not want to be the reason for isolating Gautam from his parents, especially when they had been so supportive of their relationship. Moreover, Roshni still had her house, which they could come to stay on the weekends if privacy is what they craved.

Roshni hardly spoke to Gautam on the four days preceding their engagement day due to his hectic schedule. She had developed apprehensions about their relationship and wanted to discuss them with him, but he was not available to speak to her for any length of time. Roshni was worried and speaking to Gautam was the only thing that could have put her mind to peace. She wanted to pour her heart out to him and get his view but, more importantly, his assurances.

Gautam was all ready and, after getting several solo photos clicked by the professional photographer, he took his position on the stage for the ring ceremony. He was looking distinctly royal, wearing a heavily embroidered red sherwani with a golden dhoti at the bottom, with Jodhpuri shoes, waiting eagerly for his lady love to make an appearance. A few moments later, Roshni walked in with Richa and Sonal by her side, looking absolutely stunning wearing a traditional yet modern red designer lehenga with alluring embroidered motifs. Gautam had never seen Roshni so decked up in Indian clothes and was floored. He genuinely felt very lucky to be marrying her.

The ring ceremony was performed by a Panditji by reciting a few *shlokas*, according to tradition at an auspicious time, as given in the Hindu calendar. The rings were exchanged by Roshni and Gautam with great fanfare. There was such a big crowd on the stage that Gautam feared it would break any moment. Luckily, senses prevailed, and everyone got off in time. The gathering had also built up over time, and there were over three hundred guests packed into the hall.

Gautam and Roshni placed themselves on a sofa in front of the stage as there was going to be a dance performance by friends, cousins and elder relatives of Gautam, including his parents.

The dance act went on for nearly fifteen minutes, with some outstandingly well-choreographed professional performances by the youngsters and some clumsy ones by the elders, which were even more fun to watch. This also gave Gautam an opportunity to introduce to Roshni, all his family members who had come on stage for the act.

The highlight of the act, though, was the performance given by Gautam's parents and Richa with her husband Amit. At the end of which, they came down from the stage to bring the new couple up for their first official dance after the engagement in front of the entire family and friends gathered there.

The bride and bridegroom took centre stage and showed off their moves. It was the end of the gig, and everyone joined in as the DJ started belting out one hit Bollywood song after another.

Fifteen to twenty minutes of high-energy dancing later, Roshni went back to sit down with Sonal. "I am really tired. Even twenty minutes of dancing is wearing me out," remarked an exhausted Roshni.

"Yes, and look at him, he is going crazy," added Sonal appreciating Gautam's energy levels and excitement.

Gautam noticed that Roshni had left him alone on the dance floor and was sitting down with Sonal. He came running back and grabbed the seat next to her. "If you're not dancing, then I am not going to either," he remarked in a childlike tone.

"I am getting old, Gautam. I cannot keep up with your stamina," replied Roshni in a tired tone.

Gautam was a bit taken aback with Roshni's reluctance and attitude, which he had hoped would be far more enthusiastic. It is not that you get married every now and then, he thought. As he was about to reply, Rohit intervened and dragged him to the dance floor again. Gautam started to reluctantly go with him, as everyone was requesting him to come back and join them. He, however, had a puzzled look on his face, which suggested, "What's wrong, Roshni?" But he could only get a little fake smile from her. "Must be the wedding jitters," Gautam thought to himself as he again hit the dance floor with great gusto.

"You know, Sonal, the things we discussed the day when you had come over, about the issues which may crop up due to our age difference. They have been circling in my head, and the more I think about it, the more I feel that I might have made a mistake," said Roshni in a somber mood.

"What things? What mistake?" asked a confused Sonal.

"I am rethinking my decision to marry Gautam," replied Roshni in a trembling voice.

"What? Are you serious?" shrieked Sonal. "Have you discussed with him your concerns? Don't do anything stupid without talking to him and discussing your fears. You are supposed to marry him in two days!"

Sonal, like Gautam, was fearing that Roshni was experiencing jitters, and any decision taken in haste would not be a good one.

"Maybe it is the occasion that is getting to you, Roshni. It may very well just be anxiousness. Don't think of any issues now, just remain positive." Sonal was trying her best to calm down Roshni, who seemed to be having a breakdown as she excused herself to rush to the dressing room. She could not be seen crying at her own engagement party.

She entered the room along with Sonal, with tears running down her cheeks. "I have not talked to Gautam but the more I think about it, the more strongly I feel that I should not go ahead with the marriage. Not for my sake, but I feel this marriage with me will deprive Gautam of his youth and a happy married life. I can't be selfish with my love. It would be better if he got married to a girl his age and do things which they will both enjoy and love. Maybe Payal is ideal for him – their interests, their views match and, had it not been for me, I am sure Gautam would have been with her."

"I will speak to him and end it tomorrow," concluded a downcast and heartbroken Roshni, who was willing to sacrifice her happiness and love for the greater good of Gautam.

THE ENGAGEMENT CEREMONY WENT AS WELL AS Gautam's family had expected it to. Everyone loved the food, which was a mix of Indian, Chinese, Italian, Mexican and Mumbai street food. The party, with a heavy dose of music, dance and alcohol, went on until 1:30 a.m. Luckily for Roshni, Gautam was high on life, as well as alcohol, and in no condition to drop her back.

She had decided to call off the wedding, and it would be better to inform Gautam personally when he was sober. Sonal and her husband were at hand to give her the ride back home. Roshni had spent the rest of the party avoiding people and trying to keep mostly to herself. She did not want to be introduced to Gautam's relatives one day before separating from him. She made a hasty getaway as soon as the celebrations ended, barely meeting Gautam on the way out.

There was time for everyone to recover from the party hangover as the wedding was on Sunday. It also gave time for Roshni to let Gautam know her decision and stop the wedding preparations.

The next day, there was no response from Gautam to Roshni's umpteen calls. He returned her call at around 11 a.m.

when he finally woke up with a slight headache. The party the previous night had tired him no end. Seeing the number of missed calls from Roshni, it dawned upon him that there must be something unusually urgent. He called her back immediately still lying on the bed, with his eyes partly shut.

"Gautam, we need to speak in person," said Roshni, even before Gautam could cheerfully greet her. This put him off a bit as he had not taken kindly to Roshni's behaviour, the previous night.

"Yes, I also need to talk to you about how strangely you conducted yourself yesterday. What happened to you?" asked Gautam, in a slightly stern tone.

"Please come over to my place immediately, and we will discuss it," replied Roshni on a serious note. Roshni hung up abruptly as she wanted to avoid pursuing the conversation further over the phone.

Gautam took a quick shower, picked up some sandwiches to eat on the way, and left his place, to the protests of his cousins. He knew there was something urgent that Roshni needed to discuss, but he had no idea what was going to hit him.

After the initial greetings, they sat down side by side in the living room.

Gautam could make out from Roshni's worried face and serious demeanour that something was wrong. Roshni had not slept the entire night, thinking about what she would say to Gautam when the moment finally arrived to speak to him. She had undergone the loss of her parents fifteen years ago, and she was still not over it. Yet there she was, about to take the love of her life out of her life. She had convinced herself that it was a sacrifice she had to make for Gautam's better life, which he truly deserved. Sacrificing for your love was the right thing to do, and she was determined to go through with it.

"I need to tell you something that is important for the betterment of our future," said Roshni in a pensive tone. "We should not get married. It will be a big mistake for both of us."

Gautam was stunned. He could not believe what he had just heard.

"You must be joking, Rosh," said Gautam in a hysterical voice.

"No, I am not. I told you, I am serious," Roshni shot back.

Gautam stood up in anger and started pacing around. "How come, all of a sudden, you are having these thoughts, and you have not even bothered to discuss them with me? You have arrived at a life-altering decision without even involving me!" Gautam was hurting inside and getting irritated at the same time.

He continued, "See, it is obvious that one gets these premarital jitters, and I think that is what you are getting." Gautam was trying his best to make sense of the situation. He had just got engaged to her the day before in front of his family and friends, and today Roshni wanted to break up? It just did not add up.

"No, it is not that," explained Roshni. "We never discussed the age problems in detail that we are bound to face in the future. As I look ahead, it will get ugly, driving us apart."

Gautam had a nervous smile on his face and shook his head in irony, which confused Roshni.

"Am I missing something here?" she asked.

"No. Remember when I left for Singapore and did not speak to you at all about my decision?"

"Yes, how can I forget that?" replied Roshni in the affirmative.

"Well, as I told you earlier, I was, in fact, going to propose to you then and not go to Singapore. But my best friend, Rohit, screwed my mind, telling me the various problems that we would face in the future due to the age gap and how that will only lead us to separate. When I thought about it, I felt the same way you are feeling now. But one month apart from you made me realise how deep my love for you is, and no future hassle could keep me away from you. The depth of our love for each other can help us resolve any problem. I am sure Sonal must have now confused you. Our good friends are supposed to encourage us but in both our cases, they have driven us apart. Now cheer up, please. It's no big deal. We are definitely getting married tomorrow."

Gautam kneeled down next to Roshni and held her hand in his as a gesture to reassure her.

"I am not sure at all, Gautam. It is not just what Rohit told you and what Sonal said to me. I have seen how different we are and Sunday was just a reminder of the inherent issues this relationship faces due to the age difference. Gautam, leaving me would be the best thing for you and your future," replied Roshni as she pulled her hand back.

Gautam was heartbroken listening to Roshni, and tears were flowing from his eyes. He realised that getting into the relationship was the easiest part, but when its future was being logically debated, there were hardly any right answers, as there was no precedence. Such a relationship was not a regular occurrence in society, and hence there was a lot of difficulty in accepting the logic of it.

He was, however, not going to let the relationship end without putting up a staunch fight for it. "My future is with you and no one else Roshni. So what if you were born a few years earlier than me? Is there some rule that I am unaware of which says the wife has to be born only after her husband? You know this heart, Roshni. It beats for you, and without you, it might just stop beating. We are meant to be together. It is fate. I have everything planned. We will have two children, a boy and a girl, twins so that you don't have to undergo pregnancy twice. We will buy this beautiful sea facing apartment, and every three months I promise we will go on a holiday. I will do whatever you want me to, I will go wherever you want me to go. But don't end this relationship, please. I beg of you."

Roshni too kneeled down to come face to face with Gautam, her tears matching his. "I know there is no one in this world who can love me more, Gautam, but–"

Gautam cut off her words. "No 'but,' please. Not now, Roshni. Not when we are just one day away from getting married and having a great future together."

Gautam, who was still crying, got up slowly and wiped the tears with his bare hands. "I am going ahead with the wedding, believing and trusting that you will be at the ceremony tomorrow. I am not stopping any preparations, and I will be waiting for you to come at the scheduled time. If you don't come, then this will be the last time we see each other. I will be waiting."

With those parting words, Gautam left Roshni's apartment. He knew their relationship was at such a juncture where logic would fail to justify its future and debating those points, again and again, would lead nowhere except to the feeling that this relationship would not work.

It was time to take a leap of faith and believe in destiny.

Gautam went back home as if nothing had happened between him and Roshni. He strongly believed that if his love was true, then she would be there for the wedding and they would get married. All the preparations continued unabated.

The wedding ceremony on Sunday evening was to start latest by 6:15 p.m. It was the most auspicious time according to the priest. The reception was to follow the wedding at 8:30 pm, for which more than five hundred guests had been invited. The wedding ceremony was being held at the St Regis Hotel, a premium five-star property in the heart of South Mumbai. Since the hotel's major funding happened through Gautam's Global Bank, he was able to get a high discount from them.

The hall was beautifully set up by the decorator in a very traditional way, using lanterns in a variety of shapes and colours – some hanging from the ceiling and a few erected on the floor. Everyone loved the mystical ambiance that was created. A small mandap opposite the main reception stage had been created for performing the wedding rituals. It was meant to seat only the immediate families of the bride and bridegroom along with the priest.

Gautam was looking dapper in his one-button, dark brown, slim-fit suit. He reached the hall at 4 p.m. to overlook the preparations, as he wanted everything to be perfect for the big day. He had deliberately switched off his mobile since Saturday night to avoid any discussions with Roshni, in case she decided to call or message him.

It was already 6 p.m. and there was no sign of Roshni. Gautam was outwardly calm but inside, his heart was pounding. He kept his fingers crossed. Richa and Rohit were frantically trying to call her, but there was no response. The entire immediate family and a few close relatives had already assembled in time for the ceremony. While others were waiting nervously for Roshni at the entrance of the hotel, Gautam was sitting on the wedding mandap, all alone with his thoughts. The beautiful memories of the past few months with Roshni were his only companion at that time.

The clocked ticked away to 6:30 pm and everyone was looking tense, not knowing what was keeping Roshni.

"I have tried her mobile and home numbers, but there's no response," said a worried Rohit. "Do you have any clue where she could be, Gautam?"

Even his parents and sister were now alongside him, waiting for some response from Gautam. They knew something was wrong and Gautam was keeping it to himself.

Gautam, who had been putting up a brave face until then, finally broke his silence. "The only thing I know is that she will be here. She has to," said a hugely determined Gautam.

"Should I go to her place to check if anything is wrong?" suggested Richa.

"Nothing is wrong. She will be here," repeated Gautam in an irritated tone.

Gautam believed in his love and was desperate to see it succeed. Although, with every passing minute, it seemed his hope was misplaced.

Gautam's parents started conversing on ways to inform the guests about the cancellation of the reception. No one, however, wanted to discuss with Gautam about what had happened. It was quarter past seven an hour past the auspicious time of the wedding, and some family members had started to leave. There were a few murmurs amongst the relatives which Gautam could overhear.

"This was bound to happen. Why did the Batras go ahead with the wedding celebrations and waste so much money, when the couple themselves had doubts over their twelve year age difference?"

"I had a strong feeling that one of them would back out at the last moment, developing cold feet when the time of marriage arrived, but did not imagine that the girl would be the one to walk out."

"In one way it is good that she has not come. This marriage looked like a joke. Such relationships are meant to satiate lust. Both should have fun, then go their separate ways."

"Don't know how the parents agreed to such a marriage. Every family get together would have meant repeatedly explaining to others why Gautam married an elderly lady. It would have been so embarrassing."

Gautam's anger knew no bounds as he stood up glaring at the crowd, in seething rage. Negative comments about his parents was the last straw. He was already in deep anguish as his love had stood him up on the most important day of their lives.

"Do you people even know what the word 'love' stands for? Love is deep affection, attachment, devotion and worshipping. Love is impractical, it is selfless, it is beyond all of you to comprehend because you are lost in your practical way of living life. Don't confuse love with duty. I love my parents not because I am duty bound as a child to do so and they love me back not because they are forced to by some theoretical logic. I love my parents for what they are, selfless in their adoration and adulation of me without an iota of any expectations. If they accepted my relationship with Roshni, according to the general opinion, it was highly illogical of them to do so disregarding the norms of the society which till date I don't understand who frames. They did it because they love me and want to see me happy.

Before pointing fingers at me and my family, please have a close look at yourselves in the mirror. I know cases here in this gathering where the husband and wife are constantly quarrelling and unhappy but will not separate just due to the stigma of divorce. Someone here is getting married against his or her wish just because he or she is not in a position to go against the parents' dictum and ready to sacrifice love instead. I can go on with such examples and embarrass you all further. Do you take every decision with an eye on the future? Do you own or see the future? Do you even know if you are going to be alive tomorrow? Then how do you know for sure that my marriage with Roshni is not going to work and is on shaky grounds?

What wrong have I and Roshni done by loving each other? Are we breaking any laws? Everyone has an opinion on everything and anything. I beg of you to keep these viewpoints to yourself. You people don't realise the emotional cost of your judgements. Roshni and I are two consenting adults who know the rights and wrongs and have the authority and capability to decide what is good or bad for us. We don't need your approval.

But look, what all your opinions and pressure has done to us. I am here alone while Roshni thinks that by not marrying me, she is doing the right thing. Hearing views like yours, she now believes that a young man will waste his life getting tied up with an older woman. So she has to give up her love for my benefit. Why can't you all just leave us alone?"

The built up frustration inside Gautam was finally out. There was no villain in his story, just judgemental thinking and doubts based on the age gap of twelve years which played mayhem.

Mr Batra went over to his son and got him to calm down. Being stood up at his own wedding had made Gautam emotionally distraught. He already looked depressed and was in a foul mood. Gautam had trusted that his love would come through, but it was not as strong as he had believed. The events of the past five months flashed in front of him – crush, love, anger, despair, love again, anguish and now sadness. The myriad of emotions overwhelmed him. He was a broken man. Realisation dawned on him that he was never going to see Roshni again. Rohit walked over to help Gautam get off the stage. The longer he stayed alone on the wedding stage, the worse he would feel. Gautam though refused to heed to Rohit.

"Let's go Gautam... don't feel sad. Whatever happens, happens for the best. All your close friends are here. Even Payal is reaching in a bit. She just landed in Mumbai an hour back. We will celebrate your rebirth as a single man. What say?" Rohit tried his utmost to cheer a sullen Gautam.

As Rohit was trying to motivate his best friend into a good mood, there was a tap on Gautam's shoulder.

"Leave me alone. I am still going to wait for her. She will come."

Gautam's determination had still not subsided as he pushed the hand away. Gautam looked at Rohit, who had a big smile on his face as he nodded to acknowledge what Gautam had wanted to hear all evening. Gautam closed his eyes in relief. He had still not turned around to face Roshni.

"Cheer up, Gautam. We cannot get married with you in such a bad mood."

Gautam finally heard the voice he was so craving for. He smiled and looked over his shoulder.

In a beautiful traditional pink sari with glass beadwork all over, Roshni looked like the bride Gautam had dreamt about his whole life. She looked stunningly beautiful and had tears in her eyes.

She sat down next to her fiancé on the wedding stage and expressed her feelings. "I am extremely sorry, Gautam. Please don't ever let my fears get the better of me. I thought I was doing the right thing by not marrying you. I desperately wanted to speak to you after our discussion yesterday but you, like a stupid person, switched off your mobile. Being unable to hear your voice for an entire day made me miserable. Then, I realised how dismal and lonely my life would be, if it is without you next to me. I apologise to everyone from the bottom of my heart for coming late."

"I knew we were destined for each other. Thanks for coming, let's get the wedding ceremony started," remarked an elated Gautam. He and Roshni hugged each other, both profusely crying at the relief of having taken the leap of faith and believing in their love.

"Do you both realise that the amount of tears pouring out might actually extinguish the holy fire and you might remain single all your lives?" teased Rohit trying to make light of the situation, as the entire family assembled around the stage for the wedding ceremony to begin. To Gautam and Roshni, it did not matter that the auspicious time had passed. What mattered was that they were together now, and forever.

The tension earlier in the evening had given way to glorious smiles and a festive atmosphere, as Roshni and Gautam tied the knot to become husband and wife.

The reception was held in the evening as planned, with a large turnout to bless the newly-wed couple. Everyone agreed that they made an exceedingly cute pair.

"So, Sonal, by any chance, are you single?" asked a flirtatious Rohit. "You know, our thoughts match, and your best friend is marrying mine. Add to that, I think we will make a cute couple too, just like them."

"I would love to..." Sonal paused, which left Rohit in a tizzy, before continuing her sentence, "...introduce my husband, Ashu."

An embarrassed Rohit took off.

They say 'marriages are made in heaven.' You never know who you are going to marry. You may love a person and still not get married, and on the other hand, you may marry a person whom you hardly knew. The common thread is fate, which one can never fight. What one can fight, though, is making logic the basis of a relationship. If the future is an unknown entity, how can anyone's logic be guaranteed?

Ultimately, it is a leap of faith. Keep doing the right things as your heart dictates, and the right things will keep happening to you.

Put your heart into all your relationships, not logic.

The world will be a better place to live in.

It happens…